MYSTERY AT FIRE ISLAND

**Other APPLE® PAPERBACKS
you will want to read:**

MYSTERY AT FIRE ISLAND

by Hope Campbell

AN
APPLE®
PAPERBACK

SCHOLASTIC INC.
New York Toronto London Auckland Sydney Tokyo

ISBN 0-590-33205-8

Copyright © 1978 by Hope Campbell. All rights reserved. Published by Scholastic Inc.

12 11 10 9 8 7 6 5 4 3 2 1   4   4 5 6 7 8/8
Printed in the U.S.A.   11

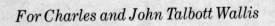

For Charles and John Talbott Wallis

MYSTERY AT FIRE ISLAND

1

DASH WAS praying for a miracle, a mystery—even some disaster like a hurricane. Anything to keep her mind off Mr. Hildebrand! Every time she thought of him she felt terrible prickles of guilt.

She stared ahead to the sparkling Great South Bay. The sky was so brilliantly clear she could see almost all the way to Long Island's southern shore. A few sailboats, so tiny in the distance that they looked like blown white leaves, leaned into the wind. . . .

Oh, Hildy! Dash closed her eyes but still saw visions of him; the best art teacher in the world, the only one of her teachers to come and see her at home a month ago, after she'd broken her leg. Maybe she should never have told him where she was going for the summer.

"Fire Island!" he had roared with delight. "What an opportunity! Don't take any paper with you, Dash. No pencils, no pens, no magic markers—don't draw!"

"But—" she had started to protest.

"Don't draw anything! Not even your brother."

"I love to draw him."

"Love him, not the drawing of him."

"I do!"

"You draw him far too much, Dash. You're turning him into a cartoon."

"I want to *be* a cartoonist!"

"I know. You're going to be the greatest cartoonist in the world. We've settled that, haven't we?"

She hadn't realized it was settled, but Hildy had grinned. "Use the world around you there, Dash. You'll be able to take in impressions through your pores. Mess with seashells, wet sand, driftwood. Do different things with it—or don't do anything with it! Just smell, taste, feel, experience—and don't draw!"

"But I won't be able to experience!" she had complained. "I won't be able to move around—"

"For how long?"

"About two weeks," she had admitted, and Hildy had roared again.

"So *suffer* for two weeks, Dash! Suffer from not drawing. And for the rest of the summer, too. Just watch, observe, try to see. Store it all up. It'll make you very uncomfortable. You'll be stuffed by September, and then we'll see. . . ."

He'd leaned over the bed looking like a great red

eagle. His eyes twinkled, his red hair and beard seemed to crackle, his grin was infectious—and Dash had promised.

She opened her eyes and looked at the large art pad propped up on her good knee. Every page was crammed with drawings—cartoons, caricatures, and hundreds of sketches of her brother, JC.

She was a traitor! Not only to Hildy, but to herself as well. If she were really serious about becoming the "World's Greatest Cartoonist," wouldn't she have taken his advice?

She flipped the pages, past drawings of people, JC, scenery, little red wagons, boats with faces . . . now there! She actually drew those boats for JC, who said every boat had an individual expression, whether humble or proud, or laughing or scowling. Were boats with faces really her fault? And was the last sketch really her fault? She'd done that for JC, too. A man had strolled to the end of the dock and back, and JC said he looked like a turtle. So Dash had done a caricature. . . .

Oh, these were all lame excuses! She closed the pad and looked back at the glorious June afternoon. She was alone on the dock except for JC who sat with his legs dangling over the edge, peering into the water. To her right was the little freight house where the ferryboats docked, to her left the pier of the "Yacht Club" with a few motorboats and small cruisers hugging its side. The sun was warm but the air was crisp and breezy, smelling of salt and good to breathe.

There it all was, the water, the air, the sand, the sun—all the impressions Hildy wanted her to take in "through her pores." And after her promise to him, what had she done?

"Ohh!" Dash groaned aloud.

Instantly JC jumped up. "What's the matter? Leg hurt?"

"No, it's just that I think I'm addicted."

"To what?" JC's eyes, which were exactly the color of the blue green bay water behind him, grew round.

"Drawing! I can't stop. It's like not being able to stop smoking, or drinking. JC! Do you think I could be a sort of—artist alcoholic? An artoholic?"

"Psh!" he wrinkled his sunburned, peeling nose. "I don't see why you should stop. You're too good. What else are you supposed to do when you can't swim or bike yet, or even walk around much? I told you before, I think that teacher's crazy."

"No, he's not!" Dash defended Mr. Hildebrand. "He's right. He says I'm developing a very strong style, and if I don't stop now, I may not be able to later on, when I want to."

"Why should you want to?"

"Because people change when they get older. They see more, and want to do different things. He's a great teacher, and wait until you get into his class. Then you'll see."

"I'm not going into his class," said JC firmly. "And even if I have to anyway, I'm not going to pay any attention to him. He's a nut."

"Oh, you think everyone's crazy."

"Most people are." JC looked in her art pad at the drawing of the Turtle Man. "That's great! Watch! I can do him."

His face fell into the lines of the drawing. His eyes hooded over and slowly blinked. He poked his stomach forward, splayed out his feet, held his hands backwards like flippers, and walked in a perfect imitation.

Dash giggled. JC got better all the time.

He passed a hand over his face, magically wiped out the Turtle Man, and reappeared, his own shaggy, barefoot, nine and a half-year-old self. Dash stared. How could anyone *not* draw him?

Long brown hair dripped around JC's ears and down his neck. Masses of freckles spread away from his peeling nose. His mouth turned up at the corners. Somewhere above and beyond his grin, glints of steel flashed like a decoration. His braces were too high to be really visible, and just gave him a gaudy, piratelike air. He wore a purple T-shirt with a large hole in one shoulder, and frayed, cutoff dungarees. There were scabs on both of his knees and most of his sandy toes. A perfect Huckleberry Finn of Fire Island. Automatically, Dash turned to a clean page.

But JC yelped, "Oh, don't do another of me! I'm sick of me! Do one of you in the cot."

"I can't! I've already told you. I don't know what it really looks like."

"Yes, you do."

"Not with me in it!" said Dash.

"Like a carnival," said JC. "Or a traveling junk store."

Dash wasn't able to walk on her crutches all the way from their house on the ocean to the bay. The huge, heavy cast had just come off her leg, and she was allowed only a little exercise at a time. So the cot on wheels, which was really a deck lounge, now doubled as a wheelchair and was their answer to life outdoors.

The back could be lowered or raised, and it was extremely colorful, with a blue mattress and bright orange pillow. A flower-patterned, fringed sunshade had been attached to the back and bobbed overhead. Bags sprouted everywhere; beach bags, shopping bags, knapsacks, a tall duffel bag that held JC's fishing pole and crab net. The rest contained towels and sweatshirts, hats, sandwiches and sodas—and all of Dash's art equipment. A small plastic pouch held JC's bait, a mess of small silvery fish that smelled in the sun. Another tiny paper bag contained playing cards and clothes pins. JC liked to attach the cards to the cot's wheels, so it made a terrific clatter when it rolled.

Dash was in the middle of all this, small and round —rounder than usual from a month's lack of exercise. She was nicely tanned all over except for one leg. She, too, wore cutoff dungarees and an old floppy yellow shirt. Her brown hair was pulled up in a topknot where it stuck straight up like a stiff brush, or a strange bunch of Indian feathers.

Leaning against the cot were two crutches, on which Dash had painted, in vivid magic markers:

This crutch belongs to Darcy Littlewood, Age 11, Fair Harbor, Fire Island, N.Y. If lost, stolen or strayed, please return to owner.

She frowned, thinking of the sketch JC wanted. "I suppose I could draw musical notes next to the wheels for the noise, but what about your stinky bait, JC? I don't think I've ever tried to draw a smell."

"Easy. Just draw yourself holding your nose. Come on."

"No."

"At least do your leg?" JC begged.

"I hate my leg!" said Dash, looking down at the puny, pathetic thing. It seemed to have shrunk from a month in the cast, and was all white and shriveled.

"It looks like a mummy's leg!" JC crowed. "Draw it like that—all wrinkled and crinkled. Hey, if we painted it with green phosphorescent, it'd glow in the dark!"

"Ugh," said Dash.

"Or draw it like a stocking!" JC howled gleefully. "A moldy, fishnet white stocking!" Exuberant from the idea, he climbed up on the dock rail and teetered like a seesaw across the top.

Quickly, while he wasn't looking, Dash began sketching him. It was a wonderful posture, and she was getting it just right, as he sort of floated horizontally, with his hair trailing down like weeds.

"Oh, slick!" cried JC, leaning so far down that he almost fell off. "Guess what I see. Two horseshoe crabs, a big one and a little one just behind. Maybe a mother and a baby." He added wistfully, "I wish I could be them for a while. I wonder what it's like to be down there?"

"If you had your way, you'd be everyone for a while, wouldn't you?" asked Dash, hoping he'd stay in position.

"Everybody and everything and everywhere!" he cried, dropping to the dock. "So I'm going to be a horseshoe crab now." He pulled off his T-shirt and stuffed it behind Dash's pillow.

"It's too cold for swimming, JC!"

"Not here in the bay. I'll be back when the ferry comes in."

He moved like the wind, and in a moment was out of view, running to the shallow water of the children's swimming area. The freight house was between them, but Dash heard his feet thumping up the long pier, then a splash as he jumped off the end.

"*Stay inside the rope!*" she yelled loudly, and heard him call back, "Don't worry, I'm a crab."

That meant he'd be propelling himself along in shallow water, trying to work his feet like the long pointed tails of the crabs, and being very quiet, as crabs were quiet.

Everything was peaceful on the dock. Dash heard water lapping at rowboats moored alongside, and licking in soft little plops at the sand. She heard sea gulls mewing and the distant roar of a speedboat, but not the sound of a single voice. She didn't really want to stay here alone on the deserted dock, but knew she mustn't get up now to use her crutches again. She'd done enough practice walking for the day, and her leg felt weak.

The doctor had said, "Listen to that leg, Dash, and let it tell you what to do. Whenever it says NO—you stop!"

That was one promise she had kept! But now she was bored, and wished JC hadn't gone off to be a horseshoe crab. She wanted to continue drawing him—JC, Jimmy, James Colson, Coleslaw—whoever he was at any particular moment. He loved to change names and invent new ones as the mood suited him.

JC's changes fascinated Dash. It was almost as if, while she liked to draw cartoons, he *was* a cartoon.

"Oh!" she gasped aloud. Could Mr. Hildebrand be right? Was she turning her brother into a cartoon?

"No!" she muttered to her absent teacher. "I'm not! I really do love JC."

Nobody would ever understand that. Not even Mr. Hildebrand understood their relationship. As to cartoons, or forever sketching him, JC *looked* good, and he was funny. But he was also a very serious little boy, and they were really truly best friends! No matter how strange that seemed to their parents, their older sister Candace, and lots of their school friends. People expected a brother and sister to hate each other automatically. Why? Dash had often wondered. But she and JC shared the world and their impressions of it together. They were people-watchers. Each had the ability to observe and reproduce the odd movement, the little gesture, the small something that caught the essence of things. JC did it with his acting and imitations, and Dash with her art.

"And as to drawing, Mr. Hildebrand," she spoke aloud to the Great South Bay, "what else am I supposed to do? Maybe JC is right!"

Really, if she could walk, or hike, or run, or bike, or swim, or even "mess around" as Hildy had suggested. . . . If, in fact, there were more people around, more general activity to "watch and observe." . . . Well, then maybe she could *suffer* from not drawing!

But she couldn't do any of those things yet, and there wasn't much to observe here in June. Fair Harbor was nearly deserted, most of all on weekdays. On weekends more people did come out, and then they had a glimpse of what July and August would be like.

They had heard that it would be wall-to-wall carpeted, or beach-to-bay sanded with children; that one would hardly be able to walk for the numbers of kids, bicycles, dogs and wagons. But now, in the second week of June, just a few older homeowners stayed during the week, and the only other families were a handful of mothers and toddlers. Because of Dash's leg, her mother had taken Dash and JC out of school early, and there wasn't another child here close to their ages.

The only real event, from Monday to Friday, was the arrival of the evening ferry. Dash and JC always greeted it, curious to see who would be arriving, who departing. She guessed that she had probably sketched every single person who got on or off that ferry! Hildy would be furious—or quietly disappointed—which would make her feel terrible in September.

The sun was dropping to hang like a great orange ball low in the west. Sudden heat spread over Dash like a blanket, making her leg itch. It was also becoming quite pink on the top, and the last thing she needed was a sunburn! Time for the old Ace bandage. It was behind her pillow, too, with JC's T-shirt. She drew it out, and leaning over, began to carefully unroll and wrap it around her leg.

Two things happened at once. A gull flew from a piling and soared, with a loud flapping of wings, right over the cot. Her art pad slipped and fell to the dock.

There was a patter of feet behind her, and a voice said, "Oh, my word!"

Dash looked up in surprise. And then was even more surprised! She thought she knew every single person in this community, but here was someone she had never seen before.

2

~~~~~~
~~~~~~

IT WAS an older woman, barefoot, dressed in an Indian print shift, who skimmed around the cot with a movement just like a sandpiper's. Dash had never before seen anyone who looked so strangely young and old at the same time. She had a small, heart-shaped face, a little pointed chin, and snapping black eyes. A conical straw hat with a small brim was perched atop her short salt-and-pepper curls. It looked just like a witch's hat, Dash thought, except for a long green weed that poked through the crown and bounced and waved gaily as she moved.

"Oh, my word!" she repeated again, bending to pick up the fallen sketch pad. It had flopped open to the caricature of the Turtle Man. "I've seen this fellow, and he does look like a turtle! Exactly like a turtle!" She looked at other pages exclaiming, "Why, these are excellent! Wonderful! Don't tell me these are your work?" She smiled at Dash.

Shyly, Dash nodded. She always felt a bit uncomfortable with lavish praise from grown-ups. But then the woman surprised her by asking matter-of-factly, "How long have you been working?"

Working! The word thrilled Dash. "Three years," she replied.

"Good heaven's, what a gift! My late husband was an artist so I know how good these are. So original! I do believe you could sell them, especially the caricatures. I'd love to have one. . . ." As she handed the pad back to Dash she noticed the elastic bandage on her leg. "Oh dear. What happened to the poor leg?"

"Oh, I broke it," said Dash, as if it didn't matter. "It was just an accident."

"Not a bad one, I hope?" she said sympathetically.

"No, I fell out of a tree, that's all."

"What kind of a tree?" the woman asked curiously.

"An apple tree," said Dash, surprised at the question. "We were visiting friends in the country—" She saw the woman's eyes were twinkling.

"How lovely to choose an apple tree to fall from!"

Dash giggled, and the woman smiled back.

"Having a sense of humor does help things along, doesn't it? Well, my dear, my name is Guizot. Mrs. Blanche Guizot."

"And I'm Dash Littlewood. Well, my real name's Darcy, but my nickname is Dash."

"Now why is that? Because you really like to 'dash' and run around?"

"How did you know!" cried Dash.

"Because you look like a dasher, and your drawings are so lively," Mrs. Guizot smiled. "How long until you can toss away the crutches—until you can 'dash' again?"

"Oh, another two weeks on the crutches," Dash groaned ruefully, "at *least*. And then, I don't know how long."

"It must have been a bad break, then," said Mrs. Guizot. "Multiple fracture?"

Dash nodded, "And a bad hip bruise."

"Ouch, that's painful."

"It sure was!" said Dash proudly.

Just then JC came running up, dripping from his swim, with a strand of seaweed trailing from his shorts like a long green tail.

"This is my brother, Mrs. Guizot." Dash waited for JC to present whatever name he wished to use.

"Coleslaw," he announced, poking out his wet hand.

Mrs. Guizot shook it solemnly. "How do you do Master Coleslaw Littlewood. Have I got it right?"

JC stared. He hadn't expected that.

"Well, Coleslaw, I like your sister very much. I don't know if I like you yet, but we'll find out. *She* makes remarkable drawings."

"Yeah," he breathed, amazed. "She's good."

"Are you taking good care of your sister?"

"Sure!"

"Very good!" twinkled Mrs. Guizot. "Oh, there's the ferry, and I'm meeting someone."

They hadn't noticed the approaching boat. It was still a distance out in the channel, but about to make the turn that would bring it into the slip.

Mrs. Guizot suddenly reached behind JC and whipped out the long strand of seaweed from his pants. JC jumped, but she just smiled and pulled the weed from her own hat.

"Master Coleslaw," she handed it to him, "we shall make a trade for the sake of future friendship!"

She drew the seaweed though her straw hat where it hung limply, dripping. "Delightful to meet you both. Good swimming, Coleslaw, and good drawing, Darcy-Dash."

Wiggling her fingers in a backward wave, she skimmed across the dock to the ferry ramp.

"She's completely bananas!" said JC, staring after her.

"She's funny," Dash giggled.

"She's a witch who's gone goofy!"

"Oh, she was just teasing you, JC. She's nice."

"Where'd she come from? I've never seen her before."

"Maybe she came in on the early boat," said Dash. "She just—appeared."

"Or flew in on her broomstick," muttered JC. "Crazy lady! Probably meeting another crazy."

His teeth were chattering and he had goose pimples all over his chest and arms. He suddenly shook himself and drops of water flew all around.

"Here," Dash threw him a towel. He wrapped himself in it, looking like a small, frozen ghost.

They watched the approach of the evening ferry. The dock was beginning to fill with familiar people. There were the young mothers with their toddlers sitting in wagons along with bags of groceries. There was Mrs. Morris, the real estate lady, on her large adult "tricycle" with the immense wire basket in the rear. The group of tall, bronzed surfing boys who did odd jobs around the island were there as usual—and there was the Turtle Man again—and Candy's new boyfriend Eric, whom they called the Bluefish Boy. He waved at Dash and JC.

As they did each evening, they watched to see if anyone "new" would get off the ferry from Bayshore. But Tuesday was a very quiet evening for travel, and only two familiar homeowners got off. Then came Mrs. Guizot with the man she had gone to meet.

They walked very slowly down the ramp talking together. He had a mane of thick black hair, a full black beard, and was dressed in a dark business suit. Dash instantly had the impression of a great, bushy black bear.

Seeing the same thing, JC hissed in her ear, "Draw him like a bear!"

"Okay," Dash giggled, and began sketching.

"Like a really insane bear," said JC. "I told you she was going to meet another goof. *Nobody* comes to Fire Island dressed like that."

JC was right of course. People usually arrived in casual clothes; so casual, in fact, that Dash sometimes thought everyone saved their rags to wear out here. But besides the dark, immaculate business suit, the man also carried a briefcase under one arm.

"Maybe he's here on business, just for a day," she said to JC.

But then Dash paused, sketching. There was something peculiar about that man. What was it? She had an "off" impression, as if something was not quite right about him. He had stopped with Mrs. Guizot on the ramp, and Dash noticed that he had a strange way of standing. Maybe that was it. One hand rested, not on his hip, but way back, almost in the center of his back. It made his elbow poke out in a weird manner, looking very pointed under the sleeves of his jacket.

"Are you drawing *me*?" Mrs. Guizot called across the dock. "I hope so! Come and see me sometime, Dash and Coleslaw. I'm on the bay in a house called The Lookout." She waved at the children and walked on with the man.

JC imitated the man's walk, and Mrs. Guizot's birdlike motion, and then looked at Dash's sketch. "It's good. But it's almost too good. It looks just like him, and not like a bear."

Dry now, JC stuffed the wet towel into a bag. "Hey—want a popsicle or something?"

"Yes!" cried Dash, realizing they hadn't had a treat all afternoon.

JC ran to the back of the cot and pushed it up the dock. He was so expert at rolling it that Dash often felt she was in a grocery cart. It rolled and bumped up the wooden planks to the cement intersection at the heart of the village. Here were the two grocery stores, a restaurant, the fire department and a tiny post office.

They were careening toward the market when their sister Candy came swooping upon them. She ran down the walk growing larger every moment. Candy was so enormously tall and well formed that her presence was intimidating. She'd been greasing and oiling herself and lying in the sun so much that she almost looked Tahitian. She was just sixteen.

"What are you kids doing?" Candy shrieked. "It's

almost six o'clock and I have a date. You weren't supposed to wait for the ferry, you should have been home an hour ago! Dash, you're horrible. JC, you're a monster!"

She brushed him away as if he were a fly, and began pushing the cot. Dash hung on tightly to the arm rests while JC ran beside her and Candy rushed her home.

3

THE HOUSE they had rented for the summer faced directly on the ocean. Dash and JC loved the abrupt change from quiet bay water at the dock to the thundering surf. Their mother Audrey had fallen in love with the windswept emptiness of the beach in June, and had become, as JC might say, "A Fire Island Freak."

Her short dark hair was always wild and windblown, she was spotted with freckles, she never wore anything but old shorts or dungarees, ancient shirts and sneakers. She had sunk into the island, as if she were part of the sun and sand and sea.

Their father couldn't join them until July. A former actor, now drama teacher and director, he was off on a special project in Vermont, directing the year-end production in a private school.

It was only Candy who found absolutely nothing charming about Fire Island in June.

"This place," she said at dinner, "is for the birds!"

They were eating at the kitchen table, looking out at the blue Atlantic Ocean.

"Birds like sandpipers and sea gulls," JC grinned, "and you and the Bluefish Boy."

"Don't call him that!" snapped Candy. "His name's Eric."

"If you found such a neat boyfriend here," said Dash, "I don't see why you think it's such a dumb place."

"He's not that neat. Frankly, he's kind of boring," said Candy sourly. She stuffed a huge piece of pizza in her mouth and looked at her mother. "He's as old-fashioned as you and Dad. And so's the island. It's boring. There's nothing to do."

"Grotesque," said JC, observing Candy talking with her mouth full.

"That's the point of being here," said Audrey. "There is nothing to do. It's a good rest."

"Know what we're going to do tonight?" Candy mumbled, still eating so swiftly it was a wonder she could chew, swallow, or even digest. "We'll take a little walk. Then we'll go to his house and listen to records—with Eric's *mother*! I might as well be back in New York."

"I'm getting tired of your complaints, Candy!" her

mother roared. It took Audrey a little while, but she was quite capable of losing her temper in a big way. "If you don't like it here, go back to New York. Have a long, hot summer."

"Okay," Candy smiled smartly, gulping the last of her pizza. She rose from the table with her plate.

"There are plenty of things to do here!" Audrey snapped. "You could go fishing, or clamming. All the things your sister can't do yet! If you and Eric want to do something, you could also hike to Ocean Beach."

"He's too tired, after catching bluefish all day," Candy drawled.

"Why don't you go catch 'em with him?" asked Dash.

"Because Eric gets up at five o'clock in the morning," JC drawled, imitating Candy perfectly. "And our precious sister sleeps until *noon*."

Candy turned from the sink where she was washing her plate and flicked drops of water at JC.

"CANDACE!" her mother yelled.

She smiled, waving an immense brown arm. "Ta, ta." She slammed out the back door and stamped down the steps so heavily the whole house shook.

"Teen-agers!" Audrey spluttered. She rose, holding her own plate as if about to smash it, but paused. "Mustn't. Everything's rented." She placed it very gently in the sink and looked at Dash and JC.

"*Don't!*" they said together, guessing what was next.

Everytime their mother became furious with Candy and regretted it a moment later, she would tell the same story. She'd remind them that Candy didn't share any of the family's "gifts." Dash had her art, JC and his father had their acting, and Audrey had a way with words. She was a part-time editor and writer. But poor Candy had nothing that could remotely be called a talent.

Nor did Candy even *look* like the rest of the family. Heads higher, and bigger, and blonder, she actually resembled the family portrait of a great-grandfather who had been a blacksmith in long ago days! And she was just as strong. That made her very difficult to manage. How did you discipline an almost-giantess, Dash often wondered?

At times like these, Audrey would always plead with Dash and JC to understand their sister. In a way, she was also reminding herself how strange Candy must feel in the midst of this "creative" family. Like a maverick horse.

But this time there was no lecture. "I'm going to watch the sunset at the dock." Audrey said. "Do you mind being alone?"

"No!" they cried. They loved to be all alone and pretend it was their own private house.

"I'll even do the dishes," JC offered in a saintlike manner. There were just three plates left.

"I thank you sincerely, James Colson," Audrey smiled. "Be nice to Candy if she comes back early. I'm afraid I lost my temper."

The house shook again as she left.

It was built above the sand on wooden pilings. The kitchen, living room, and the screened-in porch they loved so much, all faced out to sea. In the rear were three bedrooms and a bath. But the real shower was outside, in a little shed by the back door steps.

In front of the house a wide deck overlooked the sea,

and a side ramp led down to the walk that stretched from ocean to bay.

Dash walked out with her crutches to the deck and sat down in the cot. They always parked it just in front of the living room windows, which were set back, making an alcove. It was cozy here, out of the wind.

In front of the deck the dunes rose with a gentle swell and then dropped down to the beach. Once high, they were now badly eroded. There was a real danger that with the next large hurricane, many of the ocean-front houses might be swept out to sea. Rust-colored wooden fences ran across the bottom of the dunes, where the sand was dark, almost purple. Then sand colors changed, becoming lighter and lighter near the shoreline, as the beach met the oncoming waves.

Oh, the sea! Dash couldn't understand how Candy could find the island boring when she was able to walk and run and swim. Dash couldn't even manage to walk in the sand yet—it was much too hard on her leg. She longed to run down to the surf, to feel the tide pulling under her feet, to be splashed and frothed and bubbled—to be *wet*, all over.

She never tried to sketch the sea. She had drawn the sandpipers running back and forth, and the large gulls soaring high and swooping down to rest on the waves. But never the sea! It was too magnificent, too vast and changeable. Sometimes it was as smooth and glossy as velvet, like something she wanted to stroke. At other times it seemed to be laughing in an uncertain way, as if it didn't know a direction. Waves would crash into each other, explode in spurts of high flying spume, and then subside, reconsidering.

She loved the ocean most of all when it was wild;

when rollers charged in from far off, their manes of spray flying and lifting in the wind. Tonight it was calm. Echoes of the pink and purple sunset lingered with reflected light from the west, shining on the water, making it glow like a great spreading liquid pearl.

Way out on the horizon two freighters were heading east. Closer in to shore she saw a smaller boat with all its lights blazing. It looked like an unusually lovely private yacht, and Dash wished she had binoculars.

The house went dark behind her when JC turned off the kitchen light. Then the back door slammed and out he came. "This is the hour for mosquitos!" he announced. "Suppose a mosquito got under your bandage?"

"Oh, don't, JC, you'll make me itch!"

He sat in a deck chair beside her. The sunset light had faded and now the ocean was a deep, dark blue. When night did arrive, it came quickly. A few stars winked on and the moon appeared, making a path on the waves.

"Oh, look at that, JC!" breathed Dash. "You could walk on it, all the way up to the stars. . . ."

But he was on his feet, staring at something. "Shhh!"

For a minute Dash thought he was acting. He pressed himself against the wall of the alcove, peering around like a spy. Her cot was shoved back, so she had to crane forward to see.

A man was standing at the head of the dune steps. There was a small platform there, with two benches, at the end of the walk. Moonlight shone on his blond hair, making it glitter. He wore a surfer's wet suit, and was standing in a peculiar way. One arm rested way behind his back, and his elbow, under the tight suit, looked very sharp and pointed.

"Oh!" Dash gasped, and JC leaped to clamp a hand over her mouth.

The man looked out to sea, and then along the beach, and then pulled a hood over his hair. He took a surfboard that was propped against a bench and walked down the steps. They watched as he crossed the expanse of sand, lowered his board into the ocean, and paddled away, straight out to sea.

"Did you see what I saw?" cried JC.

"Yes! At least—I think so."

"That's the same man who was with Mrs. Goozy at the dock!"

"Guizot," Dash said automatically. "But he was all dark and bushy, and this one's blond with no beard."

"But he stands just the same!" said JC.

"I know. His elbow pokes out the same way."

"He even walks the same way!" said JC. "Did you notice? Even in the sand."

"Oh, it can't be the same man—" Dash frowned.

"It is, it is!" whooped JC. "And you drew a picture of him! Down at the dock he was in disguise! We've got a mystery!"

"Maybe," said Dash, "maybe we do! Come on, JC, into the porch, and let's see."

THE SCREENED-IN porch was a playroom, a studio, a storeroom, a nest. Dash and JC had appropriated it for their own. Candy didn't mind a bit. She didn't want to use it at all, saying it was too much like being in a goldfish bowl.

Large windows went round on three sides. Directly across the walk, facing the ocean, was a small red house. Right in back of that rose a tall, two-story round house that looked like a lighthouse. The upper story was completely encircled with windows, like a flying saucer.

Candy had said, "I wouldn't want to be out here where everyone could see me. You kids can have the porch!"

They were delighted and thought Candy was silly. Large bamboo blinds could be lowered if one didn't want the goldfish bowl effect. And besides, nobody was even in the other houses yet.

At first they thought someone was in the round house, for each night, just at dusk, a light would blink on upstairs. Then they realized it was a protective device, a timer, that went on when the house was empty.

Most of all they loved the old-fashioned messiness of the porch. It was like a downstairs attic. The ceiling pointed up to high, cobwebby rafters, the paint was chipped all over, the furniture was old and comfy and sloppy. There was a rickety old table for their comic books and games and art, and plenty of hooks along the wall where they hung their assortment of bags.

"Get down the red and white striped one," said Dash, pointing to it with a crutch, as she dropped into her favorite chair. "Let's find out for sure."

JC took down the bag and Dash pulled out her sketch book, turning to the drawing of the man Mrs. Guizot had met on the dock.

"It *is* the same man!" cried JC. "Look at the way he stands!"

"And the same pointed elbow," Dash breathed.

"Elbows don't lie," said JC.

Dash looked at him. "That's very good, JC. You're right. Elbows don't lie—unless—do you suppose a brother or a twin might have the same way of standing? The same elbow?"

They looked at the drawing and thought of the very dark man with the beard, and the young blond surfer.

"I don't know if even a twin would be that identical," mused Dash.

"He was in disguise," said JC. "It's easy to put on a black wig and a beard."

"Yes—but why would anybody here want to wear a disguise?"

"Cause he's got something to do with that witch, Mrs. Goozy, Gizzard, Gazebo—"

"Oh, come on, JC, she's not a witch."

"She's *something*!" said JC.

Dash had a sudden, worrying thought. "Listen, if that man is passing himself off as somebody else, maybe we should warn her."

"Maybe they're in cahoots," said JC. "I wouldn't tell her one single thing. Not until I found out for sure, and found out what he was doing."

The idea was appealing. "But," Dash wondered, "how could we do that? I suppose you mean sneak around and follow him—"

"Sure! Be detectives!"

"But that's not fair!" cried Dash. "I can't go running around yet, following people—"

"You can do a little," said JC. "And what you can't do, I can. I'll be your legs." He saluted briskly, "Lieutenant Legs reporting!"

"I don't want you sneaking around without me," said Dash. "This could be serious."

JC ignored that and clowned. "Why should I be a mere lieutenant? Mandarin Falcon is here!" he said in deep tones. "The world's greatest detective. That's who I'll be, the Great Falcon."

"JC, I wish you'd stop this."

"And you," he said, "can be the Great Elephant Brain, remembering clues. You know elephants—they never forget."

He suddenly turned off the porch light and flung himself on the couch, pressing his nose against the windowpane.

"What are you doing, JC?"

"Being the Falcon. I'm going to watch for him to come back and then follow him wherever he goes. I'll bet you anything he goes straight to Gizzard's house."

"JC, you are not going to follow him!" cried Dash. "And besides, he might not come in by the same walk. He could surf back anywhere along the beach."

JC was silent for a minute, and then he said, "Why did he take that board out, anyway? It's not the right sea for surfing, is it?"

Dash blinked in the dark. JC was right. They often saw the boys out surfing, but only when there were really good waves breaking out from shore. Tonight the sea was silken smooth. . . .

"Well," she pondered aloud, "maybe he likes it calm."

They waited in the dark porch while outside the moon rose higher. Dash grew sleepy, listening to the rhythmic pull of the tide. "This is silly," she murmured, "he could be out there for hours."

"Detectives have to be patient," said JC cheerfully.

She blinked heavily at his blurred form on the couch.

He was probably deep into character, every inch the Great Falcon. . . .

"Here he comes!" cried JC, shaking her.

"Where, what?" Dash started, and then knew she'd dropped off to sleep.

"Up the steps. He's coming to the walk."

Quickly, Dash hobbled from the chair to the couch, and looked out the window with JC. The man's hood was off and they could see his blond hair clearly. He carried the surfboard, and it looked as if he had something else with him as well.

"What is that?" whispered Dash. "Can you make it out?"

"It looks round," JC whispered back. "I'm going to follow him."

"JC!" said Dash, but her warning was unnecessary.

"Oh, heck!" said JC in a deflated tone. "I don't have to follow him."

The surfer was heading directly for the round house. He left the board on the deck, went inside, and a moment later a light blinked on upstairs. They could see him in his wet suit as he moved around.

"Shoot!" said JC. "That's that." He jumped up and turned on the porch light again.

"What are you doing?" Dash protested. "Now he can see us."

"And we can see him, and it doesn't matter. He can't be the same man, after all."

"Why do you say that, JC? Why not?"

"Because there he is, for all the world to see!" cried JC. "If it was the same man, and he was in disguise, he'd be hiding, wouldn't he? He'd never turn on a light. He wouldn't want anybody to *see* him. So I guess he has nothing to hide. And there goes Mandarin Falcon. And one great mystery."

In a disgruntled way, JC grabbed a comic book and started to read.

But Dash frowned as she stared up at the blond man in the round house. She could see him from the waist up and his back was to her. Abruptly he turned, came to the window, and looked directly down at the porch. Dash averted her eyes. It made her feel as Candy had said, a goldfish in a bowl. And it was uncomfortable, until finally the man turned away. She had a strange feeling he hadn't known anyone was in this house. But even if he had known. . . .

Dash said thoughtfully, "I don't think you're right about that, JC. I mean, okay, it *might* not be the same man. But if it is, he wouldn't care about being 'seen' at all."

"Sure he would!" said JC. And a second later, "Why wouldn't he?"

"Because if that black hair and beard is a disguise, it's a pretty good one, isn't it?"

"I guess so—"

"We didn't think it was phony at the dock today."

"Nope—"

"So, who in the world would ever notice that he and this blonde man might be the same person?"

"Whoo?" JC sounded like an owl. "Everybody! It's obvious."

"Why is it obvious?" Dash prompted him.

"Because, even though it isn't the same man, they walk the same, they stand the same, their elbows have the same shape—"

"But 'whoo' ever looks at the way people walk and stand?" Dash smiled a bit smugly. "Whoever notices an elbow?"

JC lowered his comic book to stare at her.

"You and me, JC, that's all! Most people never see things like that. Mother and Daddy don't see things the way we do. And Candy never notices a thing, does she?"

"No—"

"But we do, because we're used to looking. I practically live through my eyes. And JC, you're so busy imitating people all the time—right?"

"Right!" he said, a little awed.

"You have to admit we're sort of strange, JC."

"I suppose we are."

"So!" said Dash excitedly, "if that *is* the same man, we're probably the only people on all of Fire Island who'd ever suspect it!"

"Whew!" JC's eyes bulged.

Dash slid her eyes toward the round house. The man was at the window again, and she shivered.

5

WIND WAS bending the dune grass and whistling round the porch windows the next morning. Outside the ocean was brilliant blue and flecked with sparkling white caps. A bright sun shone in, warming Dash and JC as they had their breakfast together. They had awakened before anyone and were having juice and cereal on the old porch table where they could see the round house. There wasn't a sign of life, and the surfboard was still outside.

"If it is the same man," said Dash, "and he's supposed to be staying with Mrs. Guizot, he probably left late last night."

"I wonder where he keeps his disguise?" JC frowned. He chewed his cereal slowly. "You know, I don't think I want to find out if we're right."

"Why not?" she asked, astonished.

JC didn't answer right away. Sometimes he could look very old, like an ancient little gnome. Watching his face, Dash suddenly wondered. "JC, would you be afraid to find out?"

He swallowed and looked at her. "Yeah, to tell the truth, I would be."

"*Why?*"

"Because even though you say it could be 'serious,' I don't think you know what serious means."

"Yes, I do," said Dash wonderingly.

"No, you don't," said JC. "You're always making funnies of people—cartoons, caricatures—"

"You do the same thing! You're always making up funny names, imitating people—"

"Yeah, but I imitate 'em—more for *real*, you know?"

Dash stared at her brother. He actually looked worried. His green blue eyes were huge. "Well, JC, if you're really afraid to find out, we'll just give it up. I don't want you to be scared."

"Neither do I, but I *do* want to be a detective!"

"Well, you can't have it both ways, JC! I mean, if it's a real mystery—"

"I know, I know, let me think." JC finished his cereal and said, "Well, I have to learn to be brave sometime."

"You're already brave."

"No, I'm really a coward at heart."

"Oh, JC!"

"It's the truth. I'm just a miserable coward. That's why I pretend all the time."

"You're pretending right now," said Dash. "You're pretending to be a coward when you're not. I've seen you a hundred times getting skinned, falling down, banging your head—you never even whimper! You're very brave."

"Oh, all that!" JC waved a hand. "That's *nothing*!"

"Then what *are* you a coward about?"

JC scrunched up his face and stared at the rafters. "Uh—it's hard to describe. Serious things—serious people. Like—suppose this guy has a gun? Suppose he's a really evil person?"

Dash shivered. "Oh. Well—but do you think anyone would be *that* evil here on Fire Island?"

"You never know," said JC heavily. "Oh, well, I've made up my mind."

He rose and took his favorite hat off a hook, pulling it over his head. It was from a school bazaar, handmade, of several different shades of green terry cloth, with a small brim. JC wore it for special occasions and moods.

"Mandarin Falcon here!" he saluted. "Or your Lieutenant Legs, reporting for duty."

"Are you sure, JC? If you're going to be scared all the time, it won't be any fun."

"It'll be fun," he said. "I'm going to pretend it's just a game, even if it isn't. And if it does turn out to be serious," he grinned, "maybe I'll learn to be brave."

Dash shook her head. "I'm very confused, JC."

"I'm not! Come on, let's figure out what next."

Later that morning, JC wheeled Dash down to the bay. There were no playing cards on the wheels, for, as he said, "How can we be detectives if people hear us coming a mile away?"

They'd also left almost all of Dash's art equipment behind, for, as she said, "Now that we have a mystery, I won't need to draw!"

The only piece of art was the large caricature of Mrs. Guizot that she'd done as an excuse for going to see her. It was one of the best things she'd ever done, Dash thought, and she mentally promised Mr. Hildebrand that it would also be the last for the summer! Most of the drawing was taken up with the straw hat, the dangling weed, and Mrs. Guizot's smiling face. Beneath was a tiny body, but she had caught Mrs. Guizot's swift movement and given her little bird feet.

As they approached the center of the island, the sound of surf died away, and they heard birds overhead, chattering on telephone wires and branches of pine trees. Houses of all different shapes, sizes, and colors lined the walk. Here the island was low and flat and sandy. When they neared the bay there were more trees and shrubs, and even gardens around some of the houses. A little fleet of Sunfish sailing boats rocked gently at their shallow moorings. Near them a middle-aged couple in wide-brimmed hats and rolled up slacks were digging with their toes for clams. Their buckets swayed, their hips swiveled as they moved, and from the rear they seemed to be doing a hula.

"Which way?" asked JC, stopping the cot at the bay.

"Try going right," said Dash. "It's shorter and if we're wrong we'll look the other way."

The bay walk only went on for a little way in this direction, and they were lucky. Only a block later they saw the sign for The Lookout. The house was high on iron pilings, perched above trees and shrubbery, with a wonderful view of the bay. A steep stairway led to a tiny deck in front of large picture windows.

JC turned the cot into a small cement path that led to the steps, and almost instantly Mrs. Guizot appeared on the landing above.

"What a lovely surprise!" she called down. "Have you children had breakfast? Would you like a Coke or cookies? I completely forgot, Darcy, when I invited you, that you shouldn't try these steps. No matter, I'll bring down a tray. I love morning company!"

"She's really batty!" JC muttered out of the side of his mouth.

Dash hissed back, "Hush! And don't stare like that!"

She called up, "No, thank you. We were just bringing you a present."

"A present for *me*? How divine! How sweet of you!" She skimmed down the steps. "What do you have for me?"

Dash took the paper from her lap and displayed the caricature. Mrs. Guizot stepped back, pressed her hands against her chest, and cried, "Oh! That is absolutely beautiful, Darcy-Dash! It's marvelous! It's—"

"Do you think it's funny?" asked JC.

Mrs. Guizot's expression changed. She said briskly, "Of course, it's funny. That's the point of a caricature. It should be funny. But that's not all it is."

She frowned at JC and then smiled at Dash, "Some artists do what I call nasty caricatures. But you've exaggerated in just the right way, without being mean. It's simply charming, and I love it! I just knew you were doing this yesterday—''

A voice called, "Blanche?" just then, and the door at the top of the steps opened. Out came the bushy black "bear man."

JC drew in his breath, and Dash stared up at him. He seemed startled to see Mrs. Guizot speaking with the children.

"Oh!" Mrs. Guizot whirled around. "Jason, you must meet the Littlewood children. Darcy-Dash, a wonderful artist, and Master Coleslaw. This is Jason Herrick, children, my lawyer."

"How do you do?" Dash called up, trying hard to see the man's elbow. But he was standing sideways in the door.

He smiled, showing a flash of white teeth behind the black beard, nodded, and turned back into the house.

"Well!" Mrs. Guizot pressed the drawing dramatically against her chest. "You are a perfect love to do this, Darcy! I shall frame it, and keep it forever. I'm glad I stayed at the dock long enough for you to get a good impression."

"Oh, I didn't do it at the dock," said Dash, adding rather proudly, "I did it from memory this morning."

"From memory!" Mrs. Guizot's eyes widened. "Oh—well, then who were you sketching?"

JC suddenly had a coughing fit. He bent double, hacking and spluttering.

"Oh, dear! Can I get you a glass of water, Coleslaw?"

"Nope," he ran to the back of the cot. "Hap—happens all the time. Got to go." Whooping as if he had whooping cough, JC turned the cot around and began to run with it.

"JC!" cried Dash, but he wouldn't stop. "Mrs. Guizot,"she called back, "thank you—"

"Thank you, my dear, from the bottom of my heart!" Mrs. Guizot blew kisses at them as JC rolled Dash wildly away.

6

"WHY DID you leave like that?" Dash asked angrily when JC stopped at the dock.

"Because," he panted, "you were going to tell her you drew a picture of that man—that Herrick!"

"Well, why not?"

JC struck his head. "Some Great Elephant Brain! It's our only real *clue*, dumkopf! That picture's like Exhibit A!"

"Oh," said Dash. Then, "But what does that have to do with Mrs. Guizot?"

"They could be connected, stupid! They could be up to something together—if it's the same man. Did you notice he didn't say one word to us?"

"Yes," said Dash. "And I thought it was strange. Not even to say hello."

"Criminals can't disguise their voices," said JC importantly. "They're like fingerprints."

"But I don't think they could be connected,"said Dash. "Mrs. Guizot acted so normal, introducing us, giving us his name—"

"Normal!" JC stared at Dash. "She's not normal. She's batty as a blowfish. She puffs way up and sinks down again. And she pretends! She pretends even more than I do."

"But she's so sweet—"

"Sure, like a cobra, a shark, a little black rat. Did you notice her eyes? They're all black and beady."

"That's not nice!" yelled Dash.

"Here's your Mrs. Gizzard—" JC ran across the dock and skimmed back with a cocked head, little blinking eyes, and a small, secret smile.

It was such an uncanny imitation that it gave Dash chills.

"She's a real suspicious character!" said JC.

"I don't agree. It's just her manner, and she can't help that."

"You just like her because she knows something about *art*," said JC pointedly.

"Well," Dash paused. "People who are sensitive about art usually aren't criminals! So there. We should be worried about her instead. She could be his victim."

"She's batty enough," muttered JC, insisting on

having the last word about Mrs. Guizot. "Okay, what now?"

The wind was growing stronger and whipping up white caps on the bay. It snapped the canvas sunshade above the cot and set the fringe rustling. Dash found it difficult to think with everything in motion.

She got out of the cot with her crutches to do some practice walking on the dock. JC moved beside her, step by step. "Well," she pondered, "we have to find out about *him*—but how? We can't exactly pull his beard, to see if it comes off."

JC snorted. "Spirit gum. It's pretty good stuff."

"And maybe it's a real beard, anyway. I know!" she suddenly cried. "Let's try to find out who the man in the round house is supposed to be. It's been empty all this time, so somebody should know who rented it. Who that blonde man is, or says he is—"

"Good thinking!" JC bowed. "Let's ask the real estate agent."

"Mrs. Morris?" Dash frowned. "But she'd wonder why we're asking—"

"Then let's ask at the stores."

"On what excuse?" insisted Dash.

"Just curiosity," grinned JC. "Just gossip."

They'd walked to the head of the dock, and Dash plopped down on a bench. She wished her leg didn't feel so weak after just a little walking. "Wait a minute, JC, I have to rest it."

As they waited, the answer to their problem walked out from one of the stores. "Eric!" Dash called to him, and whispered to JC, "We don't need any special excuse for him."

Candy's boyfriend, the Bluefish Boy, was so handsome that Dash couldn't understand how Candy found him boring. He was tall and tanned, with marvelous ocean crinkles around his blue eyes.

"Hi, Dash, how's the leg?" he asked. Great whiffs of bluefish exuded from him.

Dash rather liked Eric's fishy smell. He was up every day at dawn to catch the fish which he sold to the stores where they turned up later, neatly wrapped and terribly expensive. He was helping with his own college expenses. His parents had owned their house here for years and years, and were part of the summer "regulars." Eric knew everything about everybody in the community, Dash thought.

"Oh, leg's fine," she smiled. "How's business?"

"Great! Had a good morning. Hi, Coleslaw."

"Hi!" JC grinned.

"Why aren't you drawing?" Eric asked Dash curiously.

"What?" she looked at him dumbly.

"Where's the old sketch pad? You look strange without it."

"I do?"

"Never saw you without it before," he smiled. "What's up?"

Did it really look as if something was "up"? Then it might not be such a good idea to pretend this was just gossip. Instead, Dash said, "We wondered if maybe somebody sneaked into the round house last night. There was this fellow with a surfboard—"

"About my size?" asked Eric. "Blond hair?"

Dash and JC nodded.

"Oh, that's Dan Alexander and he owns the house. Don't worry about him."

"Are you sure?" asked Dash. "Does he even surf at night?"

"Surfs all the time, day and night!" laughed Eric. "That's Dan all right."

"Would he have a brother?" asked Dash.

"Not that I know of," said Eric with surprise. "No, he doesn't have any relatives, far as I know. Say, what are you two, anyway? The local watchdogs? What's all this fascination with Dan Alexander?"

Dash didn't know what to say, but JC suddenly blurted, "Oh, it's not him. It's the *house*. We like it. Do you know if he's rented it yet for July and August?"

"Oh," Eric smiled. "Yeah, everybody likes that house. But you already have yours, you know, and people don't usually move around like that. Anyway, he's not going to rent it this year. Why don't you ask him about next summer?"

"Is he a good friend of yours? Could you ask him for us?" Dash was thinking what a great excuse this would be, if the man ever saw them watching the round house.

"No," Eric shook his head. "I don't know him well. We just wave to each other when we pass. Only thing is, if you ever do rent that house, prepare to be hated."

"Hated! Why?" asked JC.

"Because Dan hates all renters!" Eric laughed. "It's an island joke."

"Why?" asked Dash.

"The why kids! You really want to hear all this gossip?"

"Yes!" they nodded together.

"Well, you see Dan hates to ever rent that house. He

likes to surf, and he'd like to stay all summer. But he always has to rent it during July and August, in order to keep paying for it."

"What do you mean?" asked Dash. "You said he owns it."

"Sure, but he still has a lot of payments to make. Lots of people help pay their taxes and mortgages like that, by renting. Dan's just unique because he hates to do it so much. He's nuts about water and surfing. So he grumbles and complains, everybody says, and he hates renters."

"I should think he'd love 'em!" said JC.

"Look, I've got to take a shower," Eric said. "I stink a little."

"A lot!" JC grinned.

Eric gave him a mock punch.

"It smells good," said Dash.

"Tell Candy I'll see her later." Eric walked off leaving a trace of bluefish in the air.

"Hm!" said Dash and JC together.

They sat for a moment thinking. Then JC asked, "Want to walk back to the cot? Or shall I bring it to you?"

"Walk." Dash took her crutches again and slowly moved down the dock, deep in thought. "Did you hear something funny in that story, JC?"

"Something fishy," he nodded.

"Eric says he *has* to rent the place to pay for it—"

"And this summer he's not renting," said JC.

"So where'd he get the money he needs?" mused Dash. "Say, don't lawyers have a lot of power over people?"

"In the movies they do."

"Well, if he's passing himself off as Mrs. Guizot's lawyer, maybe he's getting it from her—charging her a false fee or something."

"Or," said JC, squinting out at the white caps on the bay, "maybe she's giving it to him for a reason."

"JC, why are you so suspicious of her?"

"You don't see her the way I do." He leaned down when Dash got back into the cot and looked into her eyes. "You see her as a—a *nice* crazy lady. But I don't. To me there's something—uh, what's that word? Sin—?"

"Sinister?"

"Right! To me she's a sinister crazy lady!"

"I don't even think she's especially crazy," said Dash, troubled to disagree with JC about anything. They usually saw people exactly the same way.

She looked at the frothy little white caps that tumbled over the bay. Puffy clouds sailed fast and high in the wind. "And suppose I'm right and you're wrong? Suppose he's up to something terrible? JC, don't you really think we ought to warn her?"

"No!"

"We could just tell her what we've seen and let her figure it out?"

"No!"

"Or maybe we should tell mother what we suspect—"

"NO!" JC shook his head wildly. His hair blew back like streamers in the wind, and his shirt billowed behind him. "We've got to keep it to ourselves. Our own private mystery!"

"But—"

"*Please* don't tell anybody," JC begged. "*Please?*"

"It's just that I'd hate to see her get into real trouble because we didn't warn her," said Dash.

"But *we* could be in trouble if we do!" said JC. "Promise you won't tell old Gizzard anything, Dash—please?"

"Oh, all right," she said uneasily.

"We have to get more proof it's the same man, anyway," said JC. "Nobody'd believe us now, no matter what we said."

Dash had to agree with that! "I suppose you're right, but *how* are we going to prove it?"

"Keep an eye on the round house, to begin with," JC suggested. "And watch for that Dan Alexander—"

"And if we see him surfing," Dash cried excitedly, "you can run down to The Lookout and see if Mr. Herrick's gone!"

"Onward!" said JC, turning the cot.

"Excelsior!" Dash waved a crutch and braced herself for a Roman chariot ride home.

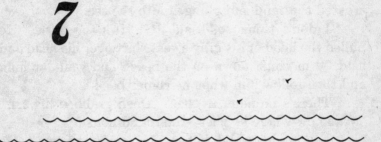

2

THEY SAT in the alcove that night with the house dark behind them. Candy had left with Eric, and their mother had gone to visit Mrs. Morris. The ocean was rough. Large waves rose and crashed, while the moon ducked in and out of heavy gray clouds. They hadn't seen the man in the round house all afternoon or evening, and it was dark, with only the small timing light on.

"If that Dan Alexander likes to surf so much," Dash whispered to JC, "why didn't we see him out there all afternoon?"

"Because he's down at Gizzard's," said JC. "In the old black beard."

Then they heard a bang. And there he was again, with his surfboard, on the dune steps. He looked up and down the beach, exactly as he had last night, and then looked directly at their house.

"Do you think he saw us?" Dash said, after he'd crossed the sand and plunged into the sea.

"I don't think so," said JC. "It's too dark." He pulled the hood of his gray sweat shirt over his head and said, "I'm going down on the beach and wait for him, and then follow him when he comes back."

"There's no point in that!" Dash grabbed his arm. "We know where he goes—the round house."

"Last night he did, but maybe tonight he won't. He didn't know we were here last night, at least when he took the board out. Tonight he may go right back to old Gizzard's. I want to catch him when he gets into that disguise."

"You can't! If he changes like that, it must be inside somewhere."

"Then I'll find out where!" said JC dramatically.

"Well, if you're going to follow him, I am, too!" said Dash firmly.

"You can't walk through the sand!" said JC. "Remember? You're on crutches."

"Then I'll sit up there on the dune steps, on the bench. That'll make it look more natural, anyway, if you're down on the beach."

"Okay," JC agreed promptly. "You can be natural, but I'm going to be the Great Falcon and blend with the sand." He pushed his arms into his sleeves Chinese style, and slunk off like a small gray wraith.

Dash walked carefully with her crutches across the planks of the deck, and had a bit of difficulty manuevering down the ramp. She finally hopped, holding on to the rail, crutches in her other hand. She hopped up the few steps to the bench in the same way, and sat down. Oh, if only she could run down there to the beach with JC! For the first time she was really mad that she'd broken her leg. She'd accepted it for a whole month now, cast and crutches and Ace bandage . . . feeling it was all her fault to have been so stupid that she slipped from the tree. But now, at a time like this. . . .

Dash sighed. There was nothing she could do about it now. But she would never climb so high again!

The wind was strong up here, whipping her hair. Like JC, she pulled up her hood and huddled against the bench corner. If Mr. Dan Alexander—or whoever he was—came back this way, he'd see her with her leg up on the bench, enjoying the evening breeze. She scanned the beach but couldn't see JC anywhere. She couldn't make out the surfer, either, in the rough ocean. There were only the lights of trawlers, way out, and two smaller boats heading west.

Wasn't it risky, Dash thought, for anyone to surf alone in such a rough sea? And he'd gone out last night in that too calm water. Well, Eric said he liked to surf—but why not all afternoon? Maybe he'd gone to another part of the beach—no, the board had been there on the deck of the house. Oh, he'd probably just been away for the day! Dash began to think that she and JC must be crazy.

A long, long time passed while the wind grew even

stronger and Dash shivered with cold. Where was JC? She began to worry, thinking of him down on the cold sand.

Then she saw the surfer. He came in lying down on his board, on a large wave, directly in front of the round house. The moon disappeared behind the clouds, and for a time everything was dark. Then she saw him again, walking straight toward the dune steps. And he saw her sitting there! For a moment he stood still, and then came right on across the sand, carrying his board under one arm and something else in his other hand, she thought. It was too dark to make anything out clearly. He suddenly swerved, walking to the fence that ran below the dune on the other side of the walk. There he dropped his surfboard and sat down. Looking down, Dash could barely perceive his dim form crouched against the wind.

She waited and waited. Why didn't he get up and come back to the walk? There wasn't a sign of JC, either. Her teeth began to chatter from the cold. No sensible person would stay out for long in this wind. . . .

"And that means me, too!" she realized. It couldn't look very "natural" for her to stay up on the dune steps. Maybe he was waiting for her to leave!

Elaborately, in case he was watching her, Dash stretched her arms as if she were yawning, then rose and took a "last gulp" of fresh air. She hopped down to the walk and then limped back to the house on her crutches. She turned on the living room light, but then sat in the dark porch to watch.

And there he came, with his surfboard! Again to the round house, where he propped the surfboard on the deck, and again, a moment later, the lights blazed on upstairs. She saw him at the window, looking out to sea, and then he disappeared.

Where was JC! She grew more and more uneasy as time passed. The house was so silent the surf sounded like thunder. She began to wish Candy or her mother would come home, to go out and search for him. It had been much too long a time. . . .

She squealed with fright when JC suddenly popped up beside her. He hadn't come in by the porch, but by the back door, creeping so silently that she hadn't heard him. But his bare feet were the only silent thing about JC. The rest of him was shaking with excitement.

"Shh!" he clamped a sandy hand over her mouth when she jumped and yelped. He had turned off the living room light and she couldn't even see him. "Come into your room," he whispered, handing her the crutches.

She hobbled through the dark house to the bedroom she shared with Candy. Even there JC wouldn't turn on a light. "Let him think we're asleep," he panted, sitting on Candy's bed. "Did you see him? Did you see him when he came back? Did you see what he had with him? Or didn't have with him—*then*?"

"Calm down, JC!" He sounded hoarse and wound up tight as a spring.

"I followed him all the way!" he squeaked. "I saw the whole thing! You don't know what happened!"

"Whoa!" said Dash, but JC's words tumbled all over each other.

"I was going to hide in the sand, but then I thought he might see me—even *step* on me—when he came in. So know what I did? I hid up on the lifeguard's platform."

"You can't *hide* up there!" The lookout platform,

some distance down the beach, rose high above the sand and had no shelter at all.

"Well, you didn't see me, did you? Neither did he! I'm all gray—I blended in. Then, when I saw him surfing back, I climbed down and waited, flat, in the sand. Then I crawled behind him—I was real close—even when he dumped the surfboard and sat there. You know what he had besides the board? Know what he hid in the sand—what he went back to get, later?"

"That thing he was carrying?" said Dash. "What was it? I couldn't see—but he didn't have anything later—"

"Wait, wait, I want to tell you the whole thing. First he had it, see? Then he *hid* it in the sand. Then he went to the round house with just the board. Then, later, he went back to the beach to get it. I was right behind him all the way!"

"*Where*? I didn't see you."

"Because I came in by the next walk, and by the back of the round house, and I hid underneath until he went out again."

Dash didn't understand. "I didn't see him go out again, and I was watching the whole time."

"He went out the back way!" JC hissed. "That house has outside stairs going all the way up, and a back door upstairs. You can't see it from here—"

"What did he *hide?*" begged Dash.

"Wait! And when he went back to get it, he went by another walk, and came in again the back way, and took it in upstairs."

"*What was it?*"

JC paused. He took a deep breath. He said, "You're not going to believe this, but it's true."

"WHAT?"

"A scuba tank," said JC.

Dash blinked. She couldn't believe it! It didn't make any sense. "Why would he hide a scuba tank?" She breathed.

"Why did he even *have* a scuba tank!" cried JC. "I know why he hid it—because you were sitting there. He didn't want you to see it."

Dash shivered. He *had* stopped when he saw her sitting there. And then he had changed direction to stop and wait by the fence. But this was so peculiar. . . .

"People don't—they don't go scuba diving from surfboards, do they?" she wondered aloud.

" 'Course they don't! And what's more, he didn't take a tank with him when he went out."

"Maybe that's what he was carrying last night, too, when he came back," said Dash. "Remember that round thing?"

"Right!" crowed JC. "And the reason he didn't hide it then is because he didn't know we were here! Remember, the house was all dark?"

"But," Dash frowned, "a scuba tank—where would he get it, and why?"

"And why wouldn't he want anybody to see it?" JC was so excited he shook himself. Dash heard sand pouring from him and rattling on the floor. "I know why! Great Falcon! Great Detective! I've solved the mystery."

"Okay—*why*?"

" 'Cause he's diving for sunken treasure! And he doesn't want anyone to know. I'll bet there's a whole gang, and they surf out from different parts of the beach—and they meet a boat—and get their tanks—and go diving."

"Oh, that's right out of a movie, JC!"

"No! Truth is stranger than fiction, and you know what Daddy says: 'All the world's a stage!' "

Dash thought about it, and then said, "So why didn't he leave his tank on the boat?"

"I've got that figured out, too," said JC. "He couldn't leave it—because he lost the boat."

"That's ridiculous! How could you lose a whole boat?"

"Easy! It's very dark out there. And the boat wouldn't have lights, because they wouldn't want to be seen. So when he came up, he couldn't find the boat—bingo! He had to bring the tank in."

Dash thought again. "He wouldn't have lost a boat last night, it was too calm and clear. Besides, why wouldn't he lose a surfboard, too?"

"Huh?"

"Well, he wouldn't leave a surfboard floating around on the water. If your theory's true, the 'gang' would leave their surfboards on the boat when they went diving. So he would have come in with *only* the scuba tank."

"Oh," murmured JC. Dash could almost hear him puzzling in the dark. "Well—something happened!" he said. "I'm going out and wait under his house again. Maybe he'll try to sneak down to old Gizzard's. I'll bet she's the leader of the gang!"

"You can't do that!" She grabbed for him. The room

was pitch black and she missed. "What will Mother say if she finds you gone?"

"I'll stuff a pillow in my bunk!" he said wildly.

"Don't you know she gives you a kiss every night after you're asleep? Suppose she finds she's kissing a pillow?"

"Oh," said JC again.

"Sit down!" Dash commanded, and thought she heard him sit. "Now be reasonable. You'll just catch a cold and cause lots of trouble."

She visualized him creeping after the blonde man before, crawling on his stomach, hiding underneath the round house—and suddenly Dash was scared. "Are you sure he didn't see you following him, JC?"

"Positive! And even if he did," added JC, "he'd just think I was some sort of beach monster flopping around in the sand."

Beach monster! Dash switched on the bedside light before he could stop her, and blinked with disbelief. He sat on Candy's bed plastered head to toe with sand. He was crusted like a sand statue. His eyebrows were gray, he even had sand on his *teeth*! He grinned sheepishly at her.

"Were you scared out there?" she demanded.

"Petrified!" he answered proudly. "But I found something out—it's real fun to be scared like that."

There was sand on the bed, on the floor; the room looked like a beach. "Clean it up before Candy gets back," said Dash, "or you'll really have something to be scared about!"

"And tomorrow," JC urged, "let's go back to Gizzard's and see if the Bear Man's there again."

8

BUT THEY couldn't leave the house the next morning. Thursday dawned in a damp, gray way. The ocean looked angry and masses of heavy rain clouds moved swiftly in from the bay. A few drops splattered loudly, and then there was a downpour. Rivers of rain rolled down the windowpanes.

Audrey was delighted. It washed off accumulated salt from the sea and made window cleaning easier. Nothing ever kept her from her morning walks, so off she went, barefoot, covered with a yellow slicker, to scavenge along the beach. "But don't you go out until it clears," she warned the children. "You're catching a cold, JC, so stay in unless the sun comes out."

Rain always made Candy sleep harder, and Dash and JC didn't hear a peep from her. They stayed on the porch, wrapped in sweaters against the cold, rainy morning. The surfboard was still on the deck of the round house.

"I dreamed about it last night," said JC.

"So did I," said Dash.

"I dreamed about drowning," JC shuddered. "That guy took me way out on his board, and then pulled me down to the bottom of the ocean. It was creepy! And guess who was waiting for me down there? Only she didn't look like a witch, she looked like a sea serpent. A sea serpent in a straw hat. And she coiled around, and wouldn't let me go—ugh!" JC shivered. "It was terrible."

"I dreamed about the surfboard," said Dash. "It had little feet—sort of sprouted them, and then ran all by itself down to the ocean. Then there were lots of other surfboards, and they all had feet and tiny arms, and that man, Dan Alexander, was telling them where to go. Like an orchestra conductor."

JC stared at her. "That's not such a scary dream. That's kind of nice. And I'll bet I know where it came from—my idea about the sunken treasure gang."

"But that just doesn't make sense, JC!" Dash sighed.

"Sure it does. Somehow!" He picked up their copy of the *Fire Island Guide* and thrust the booklet under Dash's nose. "Read it! It says there were real pirates here, way back. And shipwreckers, too. They used the island to wreck boats and then steal the loot. That's how the island got its name."

"Maybe—" said Dash, reading the section JC pointed out. "And maybe not." She read that some people thought it was called Fire Island because of the huge fires whalers used to build, when the island was used as a whaling station. But others thought the name was just a mistake; that it might once have been called Five Islands. It hadn't always been one long beach, but five separate islands, cut by inlets from ocean to bay. Then, little by little, sand had accumulated in the passages.

"They used to build those big fires on the beach to lure in ships, too, when they didn't know where they were going," said JC.

"But that has nothing to do with surfboards and a scuba tank," said Dash.

"It does, too, because there're so many wrecks out there!" said JC. "Look—read it."

Besides all the shipwrecking long ago, Dash read, the offshore reef had also caused over two hundred ships to sink.

"Imagine what's down there in the ocean," JC's eyes gleamed, "There could be a fortune in gold!"

"Hey, you might as well dig in the sand," said Dash. "It says here that a sea captain found a fortune in gold coins in 1700. They were buried in a crock, and sticking out of a dune! Maybe you're right about this, JC."

"If I am, I wish I could get in on it," he said wistfully.

"But even if he is fortune hunting," said Dash, "why would he be in disguise? Why pass himself off as somebody else to Mrs. Guizot?"

"He's not!" cried JC. "They're in cahoots, and she knows all about it, 'cause she's the leader of the gang!"

"Then," sniffed Dash, "you should ask *her* if you want to 'get in on it.' " She frowned, looking at the round house and the surfboard through the curtain of rain. Nothing was quite right. Nothing made sense. Surfboards, scuba tanks—*hiding* a tank!—Mrs. Guizot—and a man in disguise? The problem made her dizzy.

"We're wrong, JC," she finally said. "Maybe there *is* something fishy about Dan Alexander, hiding the tank and everything. But that other man, Jason Herrick—I think he's just who she said he was. I don't think they're the same person at all."

"I'll bet you a million thousand dollars they are!" said JC.

Candy slept until the noon siren wailed, then wandered out in her pink striped pajamas, wearing her pink earmuffs, to look at the day.

Earmuffs in the middle of the summer! It was ridiculous, and they always laughed when they saw her. But Candy wore them every night, saying the sound of surf disturbed her.

"Ugh!" she uttered, looking at the gray sky, and went back to bed with a paperback mystery.

Audrey returned with two large and soggy pieces of driftwood to add to her collection, and a bag full of seashells. By the time a late lunch was finished, the sky had cleared and the sun was shining over the ocean. Clouds still lingered over the bay.

"Don't stay too long," called Audrey as JC wheeled Dash off in the cot. "It might rain again."

"Rain's nothing," said JC.

"It is when you've already caught a chill. Now, JC?"

"Okay, okay, I promise!"

"If she knew *how* you caught it," said Dash, "she'd really be worried."

"Well, don't tell her!" said JC. He wanted to go directly to The Lookout to check on Jason Herrick, but Dash protested.

"We'd never go by so soon again, and not on a day like this. I think it's silly anyway, but if you insist—"

"I do!" he said, pulling his floppy hat down firmly over his ears."

"Then we have to pretend we're just passing by."

"And come from a different direction," he said. "Okay!"

Wet sand crunched under the wheels of the cot as he turned it fast on Central Walk. Shrubs and trees were dripping. There wasn't another soul outside.

"Where could we be coming from?" cried Dash.

"The tennis courts. Okay? We were watching."

"No! Nobody plays tennis on a day like this—"

"Then the dock at Dunewood. I could have been fishing."

They had the fishing pole and crab net, so that was as good an excuse as any. JC rolled the cot down a different boardwalk to the bay, and just before they approached The Lookout he said, "Why don't I go crabbing right here? You watch the house, and see if he's there."

"I don't see any point in it, JC," said Dash, but that's what they did anyway. She stayed in the cot, trying not to look as if she was watching the windows of The Lookout, while JC waded out into the bay with his crab net.

Then she couldn't get him to come back. After at least a half hour had gone by, she yelled, "You'll catch more cold out there! Come back out."

"The water's warm," he called. "Always is after it rains."

Dash couldn't shout that there seemed to be nobody at all in Mrs. Guizot's house, so she had to wait. JC actually got a crab, and held it up in the net for Dash to see. Then, as he always did, he let it go in the water. Dash beckoned at him wildly, and finally he waded out.

"That's some cover!" she said. "If you're supposed to be crabbing, you'd take the crab, wouldn't you?"

"It doesn't matter," he shrugged. "I'm still just a kid! Can't a kid catch a crab and let it go? After all, *they* don't know I'm the Great Falcon."

"They're not there, anyway," said Dash. "I didn't see anyone."

"Then let's hang around at the dock for a while. Maybe they're in the restaurant."

"And maybe this is all stupid," Dash complained. "I don't know what you want to see him again for, anyway."

"I just want to see if he's back in that disguise."

"He's not," said Dash. "I'll bet there is no disguise."

But they hung around the dock anyway for quite a while, and it was late when they finally got home. Candy was lying on the beach in a last lingering patch of sunlight. Clouds were moving in overhead again. JC held open the screen door for Dash, and when they walked into the porch they both gasped with surprise.

All of her art pads, the old ones, the new one, were lying open, strewn haphazardly across the table top.

"*Mother*?" Dash yelled, but there was no answer.

JC ran through the house and came back saying, "She's not here." He ran out on the deck and called for Candy, who was already up, shaking out her towel.

"I have to take a shower," said Candy when she walked up the ramp. She was blue with cold.

"What *is* all this?" Dash asked out the screen door.

Candy wrapped the towel around her shoulders, shivering. "Oh, that's your friend. You had a visitor, but you weren't here. That funny woman, Mrs. Ghee—something."

"Guizot!" said Dash and JC together.

"Yes, she wanted to see your drawings, and I didn't think you'd mind if I showed them. Sorry I didn't put them away, but she stayed a long time, and there wasn't much sun left." Candy started to walk across the deck.

"Wait a minute!" yelled Dash.

"I'm *freezing*!"

"What did she say?"

"She specially liked the sketch of the Turtle Man. She thinks you're terrific and should go into business. That's *all* she said. Nothing but art talk, art talk. It was very boring, but Mother wasn't here so I had to be sociable. And I'm getting pneumonia!" Candy pounded away to the shower, yelling over her shoulder, "I gave her tea. She's weird. But kind of nice."

"She'd already seen my sketch of the Turtle Man," said Dash, surprised.

JC grabbed the sketch pad and flipped through the pages. He handed it to Dash without a word.

Her drawing of the bushy black "bear man," Mr. Jason Herrick, was gone!

"She stole it," whispered JC. "And I'll bet that's why she came here—just to steal it. I told you it was too good," he added in a shaky voice. "I told you it looked just like him."

"Maybe it fell out," Dash muttered, shaking the pad, in case it was elsewhere. Nothing fell out. They both looked through all the other pads, and on the table, and the floor, on the couch and chairs.

"None of your other pictures are gone," JC pointed out truthfully. He suddenly ran through the house and plunged out the back door, yelling "Candy?" And a minute later he was back, panting. "She doesn't know anything. I asked her if Mrs. Goozy said anything about taking a picture. She didn't."

"So she must have taken it while Candy was making tea—" Dash stared at JC and her heart started to pound.

He looked just as nervous. "I told you that sketch was Exhibit A! You never should have told her you drew a picture of him."

"I didn't! You took me away before I could."

"But she knew you were drawing someone, and you were looking straight at them. So she guessed! And you told her you drew her caricature from *memory*."

Dash swallowed. "I guess—this means he really is the same man!"

"And it means she knows it! They're in cahoots. I'll bet they're up to something really big and evil."

"JC!" Dash suddenly gasped. "Maybe that man *did* see you following him last night!"

"Yeah, that's what I mean," he nodded. "I already figured that out."

"So now," Dash whispered, "with my sketch, and

your following him, they may be very suspicious of us."

He nodded. He looked very scared. "Now," he whispered back, "aren't you glad you didn't say a word to her?"

Dash nodded. She was scared, too. "And I thought she was such a nice woman! Oh, why did she do it, *why?*"

"Because it's our only proof so far," said JC. "If I were a criminal, I'd do the same thing. Steal the evidence."

Dash groaned, and then her eyes widened. "JC! What'll we do when we see her again? How shall we act? Should I let her know *I* know the picture is gone?"

"No! Pretend you didn't notice a thing!"

"But what'll I *say?*" moaned Dash.

"Just act dumb and innocent, like a little kid. Let's keep everything just the same!"

JC shivered violently from head to toe. Just looking at him made Dash shiver, too.

"Now they're on to us," JC said, "I'll bet they'd like to make my dream come true. Or drown both of us in the ocean!"

Audrey sent them to bed early that night, and they were very glad to be there.

9

~~~~~~
~~~~~~

ON FRIDAY there was a lot of activity at the dock as people came out for the weekend. Ferry service was always increased on Fridays for the stream of people that arrived. Wagons rolled, dogs barked, children yelled, bicycles zoomed up and down the walks, and everybody did their weekend shopping, going to and from the stores. Out in the bay speedboats roared, sailboats tacked in the wind, and there was a steady procession of ferries back and forth from all the island communities. The quiet, empty weekday island was transformed.

Dash and JC felt safer here, on the dock among the people, than they did sitting at home on the porch or deck. They had decided, quite literally, to keep everything *exactly* the same. The cot looked once again like a junk store or a "carnival," sprouting bags all over. And Dash had even brought along her art equipment. Hadn't Eric said she looked "strange" without it? And maybe up to something?

So she looked precisely as she had on Tuesday, when Mrs. Guizot first saw her; crutches leaning against the cot, sketch pad on her knee, pencil in hand, sketching. Surely Mr. Hildebrand would understand *this*!

For the first time, Dash wasn't really enjoying it, either. Her art now seemed like a "cover"—like JC's little-boy cover as he sat fishing off the dock. It was actually an effort to draw. But she sketched a family pulling their kids and suitcases along in a little red wagon; she sketched Mrs. Morris on her grown-up tricycle, meeting a client, and then did one just for JC of a Fire Island Freak, as he got off a ferry.

The man looked like a composite of almost everyone who got off the ferries. An old, unbuttoned, faded shirt, ragged sandals, ancient shorts, a sweat shirt tied around his waist. Two hats; a small boat cap and a large beach hat atop his shaggy hair. Carrying a fishing pole, box of tackle, two books and a small airline bag. Dash finally began to enjoy the sketch when she got to his expression. He looked around smiling with a dazed rapture at having left the city behind, at being as shaggy, unshaven, unbuttoned and "freaky" as he wished. He walked off the dock euphorically, as if on air.

JC reeled in his line and came back to the cot. "No luck, it's too noisy for fish today. And anybody'd know that. Hey—that's *fantastic*!" His eyes popped at the Freak. "Can I have it?"

"Did it just for you," said Dash, glad to see he didn't look as scared as he had last night or this morning.

She looked around to see what else would interest JC. The ferry was waiting for the return trip to Bayshore and all the incoming passsengers had left. Then she gulped, and JC went stiff.

Mr. Jason Herrick was hurrying to the boat, as black and bushy as ever, in the dark business suit, carrying the black briefcase.

"Don't look!" JC hissed.

"But we've met him," she whispered. "That wouldn't be normal. Hello, Mr. Herrick," she called and waved.

Either he didn't hear or didn't want to respond. He walked right past them without a smile or a nod. Dash looked for the pointed elbow. It was there, under his sleeve, as obvious to her as ever. He disappeared into the enclosed section of the ferry. Then the boys pulled in the ropes, the engine started, and the boat backed away. It turned in the channel, gathering speed, and in minutes dwindled to a speck in the distance.

"*Whew*!" said JC, dropping to the dock beside the cot. He looked as limp as a rag doll, and just as relieved. He went as loose and floppy as his floppy green hat. "Now all we have to worry about is the Gazebo!"

And just as if he'd called up a ghost, they heard a voice crying, "Darcy-Dash and Coleslaw Littlewood! I'm so glad to find you here!"

Mrs. Guizot floated upon them, looking gay in a colorful print shift, with a fresh weed waving through her straw hat. "You weren't home yesterday, and I did a perfectly dreadful thing! I don't know if you noticed."

JC, trying to look innocent, rose and rested his hand on Dash's shoulder. He squeezed it.

"Noticed what?" asked Dash, trying to look like a dumb, innocent kid.

Mrs. Guizot looked curiously—and rather sharply, Dash thought—between them. "I must say I'm surprised. I thought artists cherished every one of their drawings. I was sure you'd noticed one was missing."

"Missing?" JC croaked, while Dash just shook her head vaguely.

"Didn't your sister say that I'd come by?"

"Oh, yes, she did!" Dash began a previously rehearsed speech. "Candy did tell me, and I'm sorry I wasn't there. I heard you had a wonderful talk about art. Uh—what's missing?"

Mrs. Guizot cocked her head, then smiled mischievously. "I'm a *thief,* Darcy!" She went on with a giggle, "Actually I only borrowed something, in the hope of buying it. That wonderful sketch you did of Mr. Herrick? I simply had to show it to him! Oh dear, I do these impulsive things sometimes, but you do understand, don't you? Will you forgive me, and may I buy the sketch from you? Mr. Herrick would like to keep and frame it, as I did with mine. Well! There you are, apology and question all at once!"

Dash began to smile with relief. So there *was* an excuse for taking the sketch, after all. . . . JC gave her shoulder another small squeeze, but Dash said happily, "Oh, you don't have to *buy* it—"

JC pinched her, and Dash blurted, "I—I can make you a copy. Better than the first!"

Mrs. Guizot's face was suddenly like a thundercloud.

She stared at Dash as if she had never seen her before. "Copy?" she whispered. *"Copy* your own work? Don't ever do that, Darcy! It's a sin."

She knelt by the cot, looking hard at Dash, and then at her sketch of the Fire Island Freak. "Perhaps you don't know your own skill. You must value your work! Value each original. I see that I shall have to teach you something. Coleslaw?" She rose. "Let's all sit there by the water. I have something very important to say to your sister."

JC wheeled the cot all the way down the dock where a bench looked over the bay. Dash got out on her crutches, and they sat, nervously, on either side of Mrs. Guizot who stared at the water for a time, saying nothing.

Then she abruptly whipped out a twenty-dollar bill from her pocket and thrust it at Dash. "That is for the sketch of Mr. Herrick."

Dash gasped, "I can't take this, Mrs. Guizot."

"You can, and you will. This is your first lesson. Never give your work away, Darcy-Dash, to casual acquaintances. I accepted your caricature of me to please you—but you must learn not to do that very often. *Value* your work," she repeated.

"But the sketch isn't that good! I mean the one of Mr. Herrick. It's not worth—"

"It is a marvelous drawing, and worth every penny! You mustn't copy, either. When you copy your own work, you'll lose the value. Obviously, you don't know how good you really are, Darcy Littlewood."

"Well, I—no! I do know I'm good."

"At your young age," Mrs. Guizot said, "that sketch you just did is every bit as good as something my husband might have done, and he was a commerical artist."

As good as a grown-up commerical artist? Hildy had never told her that. JC whistled as if he were impressed, but Dash thought Mrs. Guizot was exaggerating.

"You don't believe me!" said Mrs. Guizot rather wildly, as if she were offended. "But I assure you, it's true!"

"Th-thank you," said Dash.

"Now I must tell you a story," she sighed. "Not about my late husband, but about my father, who was also an artist. I met my husband through my father, who had a small art school in Paris. We all lived for many years in France. . . ." Her voice trailed away and she looked into the distance.

From her other side, JC rolled his eyes at Dash, implying the "Gizzard" was crazy. Dash frowned back at him, and without noticing the little exchange, Mrs. Guizot resumed brightly.

"My husband was originally a fine artist, like my father, but he drifted away into commercial work. I have a feeling, Darcy, that you might go in the opposite direction, and drift from sketches and cartoons into fine art. Wouldn't you like to?" She stared at Dash.

"I—don't know," mumbled Dash.

"My father," Mrs. Guizot went on, as if she hadn't heard, or it didn't matter, "was a brilliant painter. Brilliant! But he never valued his work. He thought only of teaching, and opened that art school to help others, and gave everything away! His energy, his ideas, even all of his paintings! He never really accepted his own great gift. Other people had to tell him how good he was.

And even after the art world, the critics, recognized him, he kept giving everything away. Every beautiful work—" She broke off and shook her head sadly.

"What—what sort of work did he do?" Dash asked hesitantly.

"Hm?" Mrs. Guizot looked back at Dash. "Oh, oils, my dear. He worked in oil. Portraits and landscapes. They were lovely—unique. Well—they're all gone now, all given away." She smiled, "That's what I wanted to say, Darcy. I am interested in your work, and I want you to *value* it. Remember me and my father as you go through life, value your pictures, don't copy them, and don't give everything away."

She jumped up in a seeming hurry to leave.

"But Mrs. Guizot—" Dash held out the twenty dollars. "I can't take this. It's too much!"

"Nonsense! It's probably not enough. Start a bank account with it, or a trust fund for your future career. Lovely to see you both!" She waved and walked swiftly away.

"Whew!" said JC again, exactly like he had when Mr. Herrick left on the ferry.

Dash stared at the twenty dollars. "What'll we do with it?"

"Spend it!" said JC.

"No, I'll give it back to her sometime. Keep it for me?"

JC stuffed it in his pocket. "How about that! Giving you twenty dollars for a picture you didn't even agree to sell!"

"Oh, I think she meant it, JC, just like she said. As a lesson."

"Pish! She just wanted to keep that picture, and

make sure you didn't copy it! It's Exhibit A, remember. Boy, does that woman make me nervous."

Dash frowned out at the bay. "No, JC, I think she was really serious, and really interested in my work. That story about her father was real! She couldn't have made it up. Talking about it made her so sad."

JC scratched his head. "Yeah, but she's like three different people. A smiling one, a serious one, a crazy one, a—a— Well, sometimes you can't think what people are like. You just have to *be* them."

He squinted into the lowering sun and began imitating each of Mrs. Guizot's changing expressions. If anyone had seen him they'd have thought he was cuckoo. Finally JC stared at Dash, himself again.

"She's—greedy!" he said. "That's what she is, I can feel it. She's kind of like a Praying Mantis."

"Ugh!" cried Dash. "Stop it. Anyway, it doesn't matter now. The mystery man's gone away."

JC leaped to his feet. "But he might come back! Old Gizzard made me forget—I was going to tell you. *Now's* our chance to try and get into the round house!"

"But, JC—" Dash started, and then stopped.

He was so sure Mrs. Guizot was guilty of something. And now Dash wasn't. It was perfectly possible she'd taken that picture for just the reason she gave. If they could find any proof of what Dan Alexander-Jason Herrick was up to, they might even find proof that Mrs. Guizot wasn't involved. And then they could warn her about him. Dash felt torn, wanting so much for Mrs. Guizot to be completely innocent. At the same time she recognized that JC could be right. The twenty dollars could have been just a ruse to keep that drawing.

"Okay!" she said. "The round house it is!"

10

"WE CAN'T try to get in there with all these people around!" said Dash when JC drew up the cot by the ramp to the round house.

Two women were sitting on the dune steps, a flock of kids were riding tricycles up and down the walk, and a volleyball game was in progress down on the beach. It was the busiest Friday so far.

"Sure we can," said JC. "It's better like this, right out in the open. We won't look suspicious. Unless," he added, "I have to climb in through a window."

"You're not going to do that, James Colson!" Dash got up with her crutches. "We'll just go to the door and call for Dan, as if we know him."

"We can be asking about the house!" cried JC. "About renting it, like Eric said. And we can pretend to be going in to look at it, if the door's open."

"I don't think he'd leave it unlocked on a Friday," said Dash. People did leave their doors open when they were in and out all the time, but not when they left the island. "Maybe we should wait until tonight."

"Then we'd really look creepy, sneaking around with all the lights off. This way we can pretend to be looking at the house, and look in all the windows."

It made sense, Dash had to agree, "But what if Mother sees us?"

"We can tell her the same story. But she's not going to see us, anyway—look." JC pointed down the beach to where Audrey was walking by the shoreline, head down, searching for more shells. She was headed away from the house.

And Candy had just joined the volleyball game, looking like an Amazon as she leaped and batted as powerfully as any of the men.

"Come *on*," JC hissed, and they walked up the ramp.

"Mr. Alexander?" Dash called, as JC tried the door.

"Locked," he whispered. "Keep it up and let's go around the deck."

"Dan?" she called a few more times as they circled the house, looking in all the windows. JC surreptitiously tried each one.

"They're all closed tight," he said. "No way in here."

The lower story was dark, and they could hardly see

what was in the pie-shaped bedrooms. "Let's go up," said JC when they came to outside stairs in the rear that led up to the second-story deck.

"Won't that look funny?" asked Dash.

"No! We're still looking at the house—to rent!"

"I haven't tried stairs," said Dash, looking up. They were steep.

"Maybe you shouldn't. I'll go up alone—"

"No—there's got to be a way. I know, you take my crutches." JC did. "And this is the way to do it." Dash sat on the steps, and then pulled herself up, step by step, sitting all the way.

There was a door off the deck above, leading into the round living room. "Locked!" JC said with disgust. And so were all the encircling picture windows.

They started around the front, first looking at the magnificent view of the ocean, and down at their own house where they could clearly see everything in the porch. Then they peered inside the round house living room. But the sun was glaring from the west, and they had to go round to the back for a clear view inside.

"It's just like a spaceship!" Dash breathed.

Looking in from the west, they saw a huge round room with a big bar on one side, and attractive modern furniture.

"He must get a lot of money from renting this!" said JC. "What a place! What a view!"

The kitchen facilities seemed to be just behind the bar, and they saw an open stairwell leading down inside. JC pressed his nose against the glass and then yelped, "HEY! Oh! Wow! Look—LOOK!" He grabbed Dash's arm.

"What is it? Be quiet!"

"Behind the bar!" he drew in his breath and then squeaked, "On the floor, poking out."

Dash also gasped when she saw it.

A scuba tank! But not a whole scuba tank. *Half* of a scuba tank. Her eyes popped. "A *phony* scuba tank!"

"See the other part? It's hidden behind the bar—just the end sticking out," cried JC. "It's *hollow* inside!"

"Be quiet!" begged Dash. "I see it. It looks like it screws together . . . a phony tank! Or tanks. What do you suppose he's doing with them? Where does he *get* them? Oh, JC! He surfs out and brings them back—he's bringing something back *in* them."

"Sure, and I know what it is!"

"Sunken treasure!" they said together.

But then Dash shivered, "It could be something much, much worse! JC, maybe he's *smuggling* something in. Oh—no wonder he hid that tank on the beach. But why didn't he hide it *here*?"

"I'll bet he did," said JC. "You'd never see that behind the bar. I'll bet it fell over. Maybe he didn't screw it together tightly enough, so it fell apart."

Dash went weak all of a sudden. Both of her legs felt like jelly. "Oh—oh," she whispered.

"What's the matter?"

She had difficulty speaking. "Maybe he left it like that deliberately, as—as a trap. If it did fall over, it's because we—we've been walking around the house. Sh—shaking it."

JC was absolutely still and silent for a moment. He froze against the glass. Then he gasped, "Let's get out of here!"

"Wait, wait!" Dash turned to look over the deck, down and around. "Has anybody seen us up here? Do you see anybody looking?"

Wildly, JC stared around, down at the walk and the other houses. "No, no—come *on!*"

Dash thought one of the little kids on a trike glanced their way, but she wasn't sure. She hurried fast as she could on her crutches to the steps, thrust them at JC, and hanging to the rail, hopped down on her one good leg.

"Stay below the deck," JC whispered, "until the coast is clear. I'll come back and tell you."

The outside steps led down to the sand from the deck. There was space below the deck and the house, where it rose from pilings. Dash stayed deep in the shadows while JC darted down the ramp above and raced the cot back to the deck of their house.

How stupid they had been to park it right in front of the round house! But no—Dash tried to think. If anyone had seen them, they could still use the looking-at-the-house-to-rent story.

But Dan Alexander-Jason Herrick would never believe it! Not if he was already suspicious of them—and he was. He must be!

JC returned saying, "Hurry! Now!"

Dash could hardly hurry. It was terribly hard to walk through the sand to the walk, but better than taking a chance again of being seen on the deck of the round house.

Just as they got to the walk Candy appeared on the dune steps and stared at Dash in surprise. "Where in the world were *you*?"

"Oh, just trying a little sand-walking," Dash said idiotically.

Candy's eyebrows rose. "That's ridiculous! You know you're not supposed to do that. The doctor said wait, didn't he? That's the *last* thing you're supposed to try."

"Well—" Dash hedged, "I just wanted to see—"

"Idiot!" shrieked Candy. "That cast's only been off a week! Wait'll I tell Mother."

"You don't *have* to," pleaded Dash.

"But I will," Candy shook a large tanned finger at Dash's nose, "if you don't promise not to do it again! Not for another week, at least!"

"I promise," sighed Dash.

"And *you*," Candy put her hand on top of JC's shaggy head, immobilizing him, "should have known better than to let her do it! What's the matter with you, James C? We all know what the doctor said, *don't we*?"

"Yup," said JC, looking up sheepishly under Candy's grip.

"Okay." She let him go, put her hands on her hips, and stared between them threateningly. "Remember it!" she barked, and pounded off into the house.

"Oh, boy," JC groaned, "she really likes to give orders."

"She's right," said Dash. "I should have thought of something else to say. Listen, JC, we've got to talk about all this!"

Since Candy was inside the house, they stayed out on the deck.

"It could have been an accident," JC said hopefully. "That tank falling over. But if it wasn't, it was sure a neat trap!"

"What's really scary," said Dash, "is that the trap could have been just for *us*. I don't think it was an accident. He knows when the house shakes, and I'll bet he practiced doing it himself, just to see how it would fall. He knows nobody else would be snooping over there, and even if somebody did go up and look in—what would they think if they saw that thing?"

JC blinked out at the ocean. "In half like that it just looks like—oh, a container."

"Right, and I think he wanted to see if *we'd* be snooping around."

"Why would he want us to *see* it, though?" cried JC.

Dash swallowed. "That's what's really awful. He must have seen you following him, and knows you saw the scuba tank. Maybe he thinks I saw it, too. And there's the picture of Jason Herrick. Everything! Maybe he wants to see what we'll do next."

"Maybe," JC whispered, "he set the trap as a warning, like telling us don't do anything!"

Dash nodded. Every idea seemed scary. Unless the tank falling over *was* just an accident. . . .

"If he's just bringing in treasure, or something like that, that's not so bad. But, JC, suppose he's really smuggling in something terrible, like drugs, or something we never heard of? I think we ought to call the F.B.I. or the Coast Guard, or somebody!"

"What would they find? Just an empty tank," said JC. "I'll bet he has an excuse for that, all worked out. We need *proof* before we tell anybody. We have to find out where he stashes the loot—and what it is."

"You want to do that after all this?" Dash stared at him. "That could be dangerous!"

"It's already dangerous," he shrugged. "*If* that was a trap. If it was an accident, we're in luck."

Dash looked out at the tumbling blue ocean. The tide was going out and a group of small children were squealing with delight as they chased after the froth of receding waves. Gulls were floating down to settle on an exposed sandbar where they strutted and pecked among shells and tide debris for their dinner. She saw Audrey in the distance returning from her walk.

"What would Mother say if she knew about this?" Dash wondered aloud.

"You know what she'd say—and do! She'd tell us to keep out of it, and just in case we were right about things, she'd try to protect us. So she'd go straight to old Gizzard and Dan Alexander."

"I know," sighed Dash. "And she'd apologize for her ridiculous children with too much imagination."

"And be very charming," added JC, "and laugh a lot."

"Maybe she'd think it was all just our imagination, anyway," said Dash.

"Anybody would!" cried JC. "Until we have proof."

"Well, the round house is locked if it's in there."

"Or maybe he stashes it at Mrs. Goozy's."

"Shh!" said Dash as Candy came out from the house. "Later."

11

IN THE wee hours of Saturday morning Dash awoke in her own bed with a start. There was a tremendous clap of thunder followed by a short downpour of rain. It stopped as suddenly as it had started, and the thunder rolled away, leaving only the sound of heavy surf.

She looked at the next bed where Candy was sound asleep, wearing earmuffs, covers pulled up to her nose, and then stared up where reflected moonlight made little ripples on the ceiling.

She'd had a terrible time getting to sleep that night. She'd start to doze off, then wake with visions of false tanks, surfboards, the round house, the man—and Mrs.

Guizot, wondering if the woman had any real connection with all of this.

Just now she'd been dreaming of the weed in Mrs. Guizot's hat, as if it meant something. It probably didn't mean a thing. On the other hand, why wear a weed in a hat? Could it be a signal—maybe to other people in the "gang"?

Was there even a gang? Somebody else had to be involved if that man was smuggling something in, but who? And *what*, as JC had said? What and where was the "loot"? Could he be surfing out to really dive, with a real scuba tank, for sunken treasure, and then bring it back in a phony one? That would certainly involve a lot of people. Unless—was there a way he could be doing whatever he was doing all alone?

And was that fallen tank actually the trap she thought it was, or could it possibly be the "accident" JC hoped for?

And did Mrs. Guizot know her "lawyer" was really Dan Alexander? Or did she know nothing at all?

Dash couldn't keep her thoughts straight. And she hadn't been able to talk about it anymore with JC. Audrey and Candy had been in the house all evening and night. She wished she could put things together, wished she could see a pattern!

Trying to think of all the elements together was too complicated, so Dash tried to concentrate on just one thing. The surfer going out on his board and returning with a false tank. She tried to imagine all sorts of ways he could do it, and got all tangled up. She was not a *thinker!*

It was two-thirty a.m. and she wondered if she'd ever get back to sleep. Dash stopped trying, and hobbled out to the porch for papers and pencils and pens, and brought them back to the bedroom. She dumped everything on her bed.

Long ago she had learned a trick from Candy. If Candy wanted to read while Dash slept, she placed a towel or scarf over the lampshade, well away from the lightbulb, but dropping to shade one side. Dash did the same, got back into bed, and started to work.

Maybe she couldn't *think* very clearly about all this, but she could draw, and picture it. The light, falling only on her work, cast a nice soft glow. Outside she heard the ocean rushing in and pulling away. There wasn't another sound except that of her pen on paper.

She drew blocks for a cartoon strip, as a way of visualizing things, step by step. First she drew Dan Alexander standing on the dune steps with his board, then walking down and paddling out to sea. . . . *Then* what? What did he do out there?

On another sheet of paper, she drew JC's idea—more surfers paddling out from other parts of the island, all meeting a boat with real scuba diving equipment. . . . But how would they all know where to go? How could they all meet at exactly the same spot in the ocean? That was impossible, wasn't it?

Suppose there was no gang—no boat? Just Dan Alexander alone out on the water. She drew him on his board in the empty sea. Somehow it looked more plausible. But he couldn't leave his surfboard and dive down for a tank! Could a false tank float on top of the water? It was probably light, but depending on what was in it, it could be very heavy. It wouldn't float. . . .

But some marker could float. A little buoy? Could someone on a boat leave a buoy out there for him to find?

Dash drew it. And she drew a line going down, attached to the tank, which would be far below. Without even getting off his board, he could pull up the line with the tank . . . and then somehow attach it to the surfboard to bring back in.

She looked at the sketches so far—and then wondered how he'd know *where* to find a little floating buoy? The ocean was a terribly big place. How could he find it in all that expanse of water? She'd drawn him surfing straight out to sea. . . .

Straight! That was it! He'd gone straight from the beach below the round house, and come straight back in. The *timer* light! Swiftly, Dash drew it, shining like a beacon from the upper story of the round house. It could be a special light, she thought excitedly, even something that cut through fog. And there wasn't another two-story house anywhere near along the oceanfront!

She drew him surfing *straight* back in, guided by that timer light in the window, with the false tank attached to the board. . . and then she stared at her paper.

Obviously, a boat could also use that light to place the buoy and tank. But why a false *scuba* tank at all? Why not something else? Unless, she blinked, he wanted to say he'd been diving, if anyone saw him. The tank could be a cover. . . .

Then why had he hidden it in the sand! Just because she had been sitting on the dune steps? And if anyone else had been there, he might have just carried it back in?

She took another piece of paper and with swift stick characters drew another strip of everything that had happened since she first met Mrs. Guizot, labeling the days.

Tuesday, with Mrs. G. at the dock, her art pad, the Turtle Man sketch, JC, and seeing the "bushy black man" with the pointed elbow.

Tuesday night, on the deck, seeing the blond man with the same pointed elbow, surfing out to sea.

Later Tuesday night, she and JC sitting in the dark porch, seeing him return carrying something. Seeing him upstairs in the round house, looking down at them.

Wednesday, going to Mrs. Guizot's with her caricature. Meeting Jason Herrick, JC rushing her away because she had told Mrs. Guizot she'd drawn the caricature from *memory.*

Dash put in little balloons with words, and had Mrs. Guizot saying, "Then *who* were you sketching at the dock?"

She drew a strip of their meeting with Eric, and had him saying, "Dan surfs *all* the time." And, "He *has* to rent that house. He always rents it." And, "He's not renting it this summer."

Wednesday afternoon, the surfboard on the deck of the round house, she and JC watching for the surfer who never appeared to surf.

Wednesday night, the blond man going out again on his board in a rough ocean. JC following him. Dash sitting on the dune steps. The surfer returning, carrying something, seeing her, sitting, waiting, returning to the round house with only his board.

She drew JC seeing him hide it, and going back to get it—learning it was a scuba tank.

Thursday, the rain, going out later with JC to watch The Lookout, JC crabbing. Coming home to find that Mrs. Guizot had taken the sketch of Jason Herrick!

She drew JC's frightened expression. And later,

both of them sleeping. The surfer hadn't gone out on Thursday night.

Friday, just yesterday! Back in the cot at the dock. Seeing Jason Herrick leave on the ferry. Saying "Hello" and getting no answer. Then Mrs. Guizot. Dash drew her apologizing, "I'm a *thief,* Darcy!" And asking to buy the picture she'd taken. Then thrusting a twenty-dollar bill at Dash. "Value your work."

What would Mrs. Guizot think, Dash wondered, looking around at all the papers on the bed, if she could see *this* work?

She remembered to draw JC holding the money for her, and then sketched their experience at the round house. She drew the tank, on the floor, in two halves, and stared at it for a long time.

Yes, it could have, just possibly, fallen accidentally. But as Dash looked back over the other sequence of events, she didn't think so. Too many fishy things had happened.

She shivered, suddenly cold and very nervous. But she couldn't think or draw another minute. She stacked the papers together and slid them under her bed. Now at least she had a record, her own kind of "notebook" to work from.

Dash turned off the light, snuggled under the covers, and knew, with absolute certainty, that something was still missing from that "notebook." There was something that she'd seen and forgotten. But there was no point in struggling to remember—she'd have to wait until her eyes and hands saw it again.

She closed her eyes, murmuring, "So sorry about all this, Mr. Hildebrand, but I'll explain it in September."

12

~~~~~~~~~~~~~~~~~~~~~~~~~~~~~~
~~~~~~~~~~~~~~~~~~~~~~~~~~~~~~

DASH AND JC found all of the following week absolutely incredible. They could hardly believe what was happening—or wasn't happening! Although they hung around the dock, acting so normal and natural and childish that JC said it was "sickening," and watched every ferry from Saturday through Monday, they never saw Jason Herrick return in his disguise.

Instead, Dan Alexander appeared in the round house on Monday night, and there he *stayed*. Unlike the previous week, when he'd surfed only at night, he now surfed all the time, mornings, nights, and afternoons.

They saw him constantly, in and out with his board, up and down the walk, going to the stores. He even smiled at Dash and JC when he saw them, waved and said "Hello." At night, the round house blazed with lights, and the small timing light never went on. He acted like a perfectly normal, natural neighbor.

"Too natural," said JC. "It's an act."

"He's like a different man!" said Dash. But she knew he couldn't be, because the elbow was still there.

"And Gahoozy's like a different woman," said JC.

That was a strange thing. They tried to divide their time between the beach and the bay as they always had, looking as if they knew nothing, had seen nothing. But when they did run into Mrs. Guizot, she didn't stop to talk as she had before! She'd wave and call out things like "Hello Darcy-Dash and Coleslaw!" and move right on, as if all that interest in Dash's work, the art talk, and the pictures had never happened.

Everything was different! Nothing seemed fishy or suspicious—except that it *was* so different. Their fear over seeing the false tank led nowhere. They'd been afraid of what might happen, but nothing happened.

JC made a nest under their house where he could watch Dan Alexander return from surfing late at night. There was an old bedspring and mattress down there in the sand. JC piled on blankets, huddled and hid, but never saw him come in with another tank.

Audrey even let them sleep out on deck chairs under the stars on two windless nights. And though they kept each other awake to watch, peeking out from their quilts, he came in with only the surfboard.

By Tuesday, June 28, nine days after Dan Alexander

had so suddenly reappeared in the round house, Dash decided, "If there was a mystery, it's over."

"I don't think so," said JC, " 'cause everybody's acting. He's acting, old Gizzard's acting, *we're* acting! Nobody's being who they really are anymore. We're *all* in disguise."

JC more than anyone, thought Dash! He'd taken to wearing butcher-boy overalls to look even more childish and "innocent." But they were striped vertically, while most of his shirts were striped horizontally. Between all the colorful stripes criss-crossing, and his many-shades-of-green floppy hat pulled over hair that had grown even longer—well, the effect was somewhat odd. He didn't look like a spy—but she wasn't sure if he looked exactly like "an innocent little kid" either. When he wore dark glasses he looked more like a circus midget!

"Did you draw everything so far for today?" asked JC.

"Yep," said Dash.

She had kept up her cartoon notebook of events. JC thought the blocks of sketches were terrific as a daily guide. They put the papers in a folder and hid them underneath JC's bunk mattress every night.

"But there's nothing much to draw now," Dash complained. "Whatever he was doing, he's not doing it anymore."

"He's surfing, all the time!" said JC. "He's doing that—just to fool us."

"But it's been nine whole days! And we haven't seen him bring in a tank. I'll bet it's all over. Whatever he was smuggling in must be gone by now. Nobody'd find any proof."

"Want to bet it's stashed at Gazebo's?" said JC. "And *that's* why she isn't talking to us."

The sky was misty tonight. They felt little drops of moisture in the air and the arms of their deck chairs were wet. Surf crashed and boomed against the deserted beach. It was so close to July now, Dash remembered, when everything would be different—bright, busy and noisy. She knew she'd miss the quiet, lonely beach, miss just looking at it. Soon now, she'd be able to try that deep sand, and walk a little along the shore. She couldn't wait for that! But she'd also miss this time with just JC, and sharing a mystery. Unsolved! If only they could have solved it. Things had been so normal recently that Dash realized she'd lost the scary feeling she had before.

Mist filled the beach and obscured the stars. But out on the ocean brilliant lights suddenly appeared, cutting through the light fog that swirled above the waves. A boat with all its lights aglow, outlining a silhouette of lovely lines. . . .

She blinked. That picture was familiar—hadn't she seen a yacht like this before, brilliantly lit just as it was now?

Her eyes opened wide and she leaned forward. She had wished for binoculars! When was that? Something was coming back . . . the cartoon calendar flashed before her. *Tuesday*, exactly two weeks ago . . . just before they saw the blond man on the dune steps!

"JC!" she whispered, reaching over to grab his arm. "Don't say a word! Be very quiet—but go to the end of the deck and see which lights are on in the round house. Quietly!"

He rose and crept to the corner of the porch like a

shadow. Returning to his deck chair, he whispered, "Just the small light. Why?"

"That's it!" Dash could hardly keep her voice down. "The special timer light!" she whispered hoarsely. "This is the first time it's been on since he's been back. It's because of that yacht—see? And that's what I forgot. That's what's been missing from my calendar!"

"What do you mean?" asked JC.

"That's the boat that's dropping off the tanks, I'll bet you anything! They're doing it right now."

"Why that boat? Lots of boats go by here."

"I know! But that's the boat that went by the first time we saw him surfing out and coming in with a tank. I forgot to draw it. That's why he hasn't been bringing in more tanks. He's been waiting for that yacht!"

"Oho!" said JC.

"And you were right. He's been surfing all the time just to fool us, so we wouldn't notice when he goes out again tonight. He's going to bring in another tank!"

The yacht sailed on, finally disappearing in the fog.

"But why would they leave all their lights on?" asked JC. "It's so obvious."

"That's why! It looks so pretty you'd never dream it was suspicious. JC! How could we find out the name of that boat? Would the Coast Guard tell us if we called them?"

"Why should they tell you anything?"

"Well—maybe they could catch everybody in the act! Get Dan Alexander bringing in the stuff, and then go after the yacht—"

"But there must be hundreds of yachts. Shh!" JC hissed. "I think it's too late to catch him."

There he was again, going out to surf as he did every night now. They waited until he disappeared in the mist, and then made a beeline for JC's bedroom and the calendar hidden under his mattress.

"See? It was just before then," said Dash, pointing to her first drawing of the man on the dune steps. She drew in the yacht sailing by. "And there were a couple of boats the next night, too, but I didn't pay any attention."

"Maybe they drop off two tanks at the same time," said JC.

Dash stared at him. "Then, if we knew how far out they were, the Coast Guard could haul up the other one!"

"But I said *maybe*," JC reminded her. "And maybe the boat comes back again. And maybe—oh, I sure think it could be a wild goose chase. They wouldn't even believe us! No, what we need is the *loot*."

Dash dropped on the bunk, looking again at her drawings. "Look—he surfed out and brought in tanks on Tuesday and Wednesday nights. And then he left the island in that Jason Herrick disguise on Friday."

"That's the big clue!" shouted JC. "If it works the same way this time, he'll leave again on Friday. Probably taking the loot with him!"

"But all he had was the briefcase," said Dash.

"Maybe that's what he carries it in!"

Dash stared at her sketch of the dark man with the small briefcase. "It'd have to be something awfully small to fit in that. . . ."

"Evil things usually are small," said JC. "Drugs, terrible weapon plans, secrets on microfilm, deadly germs. . . ."

Dash shuddered, "I do wish you'd imagine something better than all that!"

"Sure, it could be slick stuff, too. Gold coins, uh, treasure like, uh—jewelry!" His eyes gleamed. "Old pirate treasure! It could be anything."

"Not anything. It's only a briefcase."

"Think what Daddy carries in his! Books, boots, play scripts, sandwiches—you can stash a lot of junk in a briefcase. Well," he rubbed his hands, "Mandarin Falcon back to work."

"What are you going to do?"

"Wait under the house and see if he brings in a tank, of course!"

"That's the wild goose chase," said Dash. "He'd never bring it in the same way this time, JC. He knows we saw him before, so he'll bring it in some other way, down the beach."

They sat on the bunk, chins in hands, trying to think of something. Dash gazed, without really seeing them, at the papers on her lap. Then a number seemed to jump right off the page and hit her. Today's date! June *28*!

"Oh, no!" she gasped, and began pointing. "Look, JC, he's only done this in the middle of the week, when nobody's here, and in *June*. This is Tuesday, and Friday's the first of July. Everybody'll be here for that weekend, and they stay for July and August! He'll never go out again for a tank, not after tonight or tomorrow. I know it."

"Then we've only got two days to find out!" cried JC. "How'll we do it?"

13

"SNEAK INTO The Lookout, that's what!"
said JC the next day. "He probably stashed a tank and
the loot down there last night."

"We don't even know if Mrs. Guizot's involved,
JC!"

"Well, it would sure be a good way to find out. If you
found a tank, you'd *know*."

"Or a surfboard," mused Dash, frowning out the
porch windows. The board wasn't even in its usual place
on the round house deck.

It was another shining June day. The sea was blue and silky, the sun warm, and a lovely breeze blew through the screen door. A few people were already down on the beach; early arrivals for the big weekend ahead.

"Of course, that's the way he could be using her," Dash said thoughtfully. "As her lawyer, he could be using her house to hide the stuff in, instead of his own."

"I'll do it tonight!" said JC eagerly. "I'll go and—"

"Whoa! Suppose *he's* there?"

"He won't be—if your calendar's right. He brings in the junk on Tuesday and Wednesday nights. He'll be out again on his board."

"But where's the board?" cried Dash.

"It doesn't matter! It's somewhere. And he'll go out, and we'll know exactly where he is—on the ocean." JC blinked like a small owl, putting things together. "If we wait until that timer light goes on, we'll know for *sure*. Then I can run down—take you in the cot—"

"Wait, wait!" said Dash. "The light always goes on when he isn't in the house at night, anyway. So you can't be really sure he's out on the ocean. That yacht could have made its last drop last night! You could run smack into him!"

"Well—?" JC puzzled at the rafters. "Well then, all I need is a cover."

"It's too dangerous, JC!" Dash frowned. "And why are you saying 'I'? If anybody does this, it's going to be *we*!"

"No!" cried JC. "It can't be. Somebody's got to keep old Gazebo talking while I look, and that's *you*. You've got to get her out of the house—get her talking about art. You can always say you can't get up the steps yet. She wouldn't know the difference! That leg's a good cover for you. I just want to know what I'd say—"

"*Cover!*" Dash said suddenly. "*Leg!*" She stared at it intently. It was a little rounder and tanner and stronger than it had been a week ago. She'd done quite a lot of walking, even without her crutches now, but she still had an obvious limp. Recently, unbeknownst to Candy, she'd even tried a little sand walking right in back of their house. Dan Alexander couldn't have seen her there—how often had he seen her without crutches, Dash wondered? How often without the Ace bandage? She still used it when her leg felt weak—in fact she always used it at the dock, and Dan Alexander always saw JC *wheeling* her there. . . .

"What's going on?" asked JC curiously, observing her expression.

"When was the last time Dan Alexander saw me walking around—without crutches?" She stared at him.

"Huh? What do you mean? *I* don't know!"

"He's usually seen me lying in a deck chair, hasn't he? Or in the cot, going to the dock. Do you think he's noticed me without the bandage?"

"What are you talking about!" said JC.

"And Mrs. Guizot!" Dash's eyes grew round. "She's never seen me without crutches! Or the bandage. Or the cot!"

"That's what I meant," said JC. "It's a good—"

"*Cover!*" breathed Dash. "And that's the one I'll use to sneak into The Lookout myself! Everybody knows I can't walk all the way to the bay yet, so you can pretend I'm right here at home, and *I'll* go up those steps!''

"But you *can't* walk to the bay."

"I won't. We'll hide the cot after you've taken me down. Then you keep her busy—"

"*How?* And suppose you do run into him? What'll you say?''

"Oh—" Dash cast about wildly for an idea. "I'll say I fell down! And I'm crawling around looking for help."

"Ohh," groaned JC. "That stinks."

She ignored him. "Now, we have to figure out how you're going to keep her busy."

"I'll be *scared* if you go up there alone," JC protested.

"Well, I'd be petrified if you did!" answered Dash.

"I'm scared of talking to old Gizzard, too," he shivered. "Boy, I'd really have to be brave to face that!"

"Oh, well," Dash said, trying to cheer him up, "We're just a couple of kids. What could anybody do to us?"

JC looked at her. "Famous last words!"

They put their heads together, plotted, and finally devised a plan. It involved the twenty dollars Mrs. Guizot had given to Dash, and the fact that they'd often seen her watching the sunsets from the dock.

Dash wrapped her leg all the way up above her knee in two bandages, making it look bulky and even more prominent. "I can always say I hurt it again," she whispered to JC before sitting down to dinner.

But nothing ever escaped Candy who took one look at the mummy wrappings and roared, "I warned you!"

She hit the table so hard franks and beans jumped up from plates and landed in all directions.

"For heaven's sake, Candy!" Audrey frowned, trying to move them all back into place. "What's the matter with you?"

"She's hurt her leg, and now you'll have more doctor bills, and I won't be able to have anything I want! And I told her—"

Oh, so that was why Candy had been so concerned about sand walking, thought Dash, eyeing her sister. She might have known it wasn't any sympathetic reason. But Candy went on.

"And everytime she does something dumb, she just sets herself back!" Spearing a frankfurter, Candy waved it at Dash. "Don't you want to go swimming or biking this summer? How'd you like me to call Daddy and tell him not to bring out your bike?"

"Now, Candy—" Audrey started.

"And he promised to get me a surfboard later on," Candy complained, "but if she runs up more doctor bills—"

"Candace!" Audrey snapped. "That's enough. Now, what did you do to your leg, Dash?"

"Nothing! Not one single thing!" Dash glared at Candy. "I just wanted to—keep it warm."

"Hah!" Candy snorted. "Some excuse!"

"Let's see it," said Audrey.

So the carefully wrapped bandages had to come off and Audrey inspected the leg. "It looks all right—"

"It is!" said Dash. "And I have been walking more—even in the sand, so there! I want to get to the beach sometime!"

"Well, you be careful," her mother warned.

And JC sang out, "A girl named Dash who can't dash, and a girl named Candy who's really a lemon!"

Later, when JC rolled Dash away in the cot with the leg wrapped up again, he said, "Now I'll tell you something."

"What?"

"When it first happened—when you broke it—I felt sorry for you."

"I know."

"There's more. When it hurt so much? In the beginning? Well, my leg hurt, too."

"Oh, JC, that's nice."

"Call me Great Falcon," he said. "It's that kind of a night."

As they neared the bay, however, they grew less cheerful. Their first aim was to see if Mrs. Guizot was at the dock as usual, watching the sunset. All the June "regulars" seemed to be there, as if trying to enjoy their last peaceful evenings. But there was no Mrs. Guizot. JC gave the cot a quick circle so everyone could see Dash in her thickly bandaged leg.

They rolled by the lighted windows of the restaurant, and there she was, inside! Looking at a menu, while a waitress stood by waiting for an order.

"She's going to have dinner!" squealed Dash. "Oh, this is it, JC. Hurry."

He ran the cot fast as he could up to Central Walk so anyone seeing them leave would think he was taking her home. But then he turned left, past a few more walks, then left again back toward the bay. The boardwalk they were on was narrow and uneven. Wooden planks rolled up and down and there was quite a drop to the ground below on either side. Branches of trees, shrubs, and high weeds brushed against the sides of the cot. The wheels made a terrible clacking sound.

"Shh!" whispered Dash.

"I can't help it," said JC, "but there's nobody on this walk, anyway."

All of the houses were dark. Just before they got to the bay, JC stopped and looked around. Not much light was left from the sunset. At the corner, two buildings away from The Lookout, was an old-fashioned two-story house with a large garden, trees, and a patch of thick shrubbery. He rolled the cot softly as he could to the Bay Walk, and then onto the grass beside the house. The wheels made no sound now, and he hid the cot behind the shrubbery.

Dash hopped out quickly, but JC stood stock still.

"I can't do it!" he said. "I can't go back there and talk to her!"

"You have to! It's even easier than we thought."

"I can't!" wailed JC. He was trembling all over. "I'll come with you instead."

"No, you won't! You've got to keep her talking so I have a chance to look."

"But suppose *he's* there?"

"Then I'll use my excuse."

"Suppose the door's not open?"

"Then I can't get in!" She didn't know what to do with him. He was rigid. "Look, it's so easy. Just watch and go in when you see her starting dessert. Then give her back the twenty dollars. She'll argue about it and you can keep her there arguing!"

"But I'm scared."

"Maybe she'll buy you a Coke!" Dash said encouragingly. -

He hardly breathed.

"So be a coward, then!" She tried a different tack. "Don't go. And I won't go. And you won't have another chance to be brave—" She heard him swallow. "Well?"

"Okay," he swallowed again.

"So *run!*"

JC ran. She heard his bare feet pounding up the boardwalk.

Dash waited a second to gain courage herself. Then, with her flashlight tucked in her sweatshirt, using one crutch as a prop, she hobbled on to The Lookout.

14

DASH FALTERED when she saw one light was on up in the house. Her heart began to thud. Did it mean that "Jason Herrick" was there? She stood on the path looking up at the picture window. There was no movement inside.

She looked at the cemented area underneath the house. It was growing dark quickly, but she could see deck chairs, Mrs. Guizot's wagon—and no surfboard.

Well, it was now or never! Dash took a deep breath and hobbled forward on the path to the stairs. Hanging on to the iron railing, with her crutch in the other hand, she pulled herself up, rehearsing her "excuse" just in case. On the little deck she could see inside the living room. Empty chairs and couch—no one was there. Of course, he could be in the back, if he wasn't out surfing.

She tried the door handle—open! Unlocked! Quickly she slipped inside and closed the door behind her. Again it was now or never. She cleared her throat nervously and called out, "Hello? Anyone home?"

Everything was silent. The place *felt* empty. Dash decided to chance it. She looked out the window at the Bay Walk. Nobody was coming along, but if anyone did, they could easily see her inside, with the light on. And in a minute she wouldn't be able to see anything outside. Only a few pink streaks lingered in the sky. She dropped to the floor, with her head below the level of the windowsill and looked around.

The room had a cozy feeling. There was a fireplace, a large coffee table before it, and comfortable tweedy chairs and couch. The lamp burned from a table against a wall. Did she dare turn it off? No! Mrs. Guizot might leave it on every night when she was out. Dash would have to crawl to look around.

She suddenly became as frightened as JC. She had no right to be here! This was—what? Well, not "breaking," but certainly "entering." For a moment she was immobilized with guilt. Then Dash reasoned with herself that she could be *helping* Mrs. Guizot this way, if she were an innocent victim.

Her eyes traveled over the room. What was she looking for? Outside of a false tank, which would certainly implicate Mrs. G.—where would *he* hide anything?

Keeping her head low, Dash pulled herself across the

room to the fireplace. It was difficult to crawl with her leg so stiffly bandaged, having to pull the crutch along with her. She looked behind the logs—nothing. On one side of the fireplace was a bookcase filled with thick volumes on nature, fish and bird lore. They had probably come with the house.

Didn't criminals sometimes hollow out books, though, to use as a hiding place? She dragged herself over and began to draw them out, one by one—and realized this would take forever! She wouldn't have time to look anywhere else.

Oh, this was going to be impossible! Without looking at it, she shoved back the book in her hand, and looked up. There was a series of lovely nature prints on the walls, and off to one side she saw the counter separating the pullman kitchen. Kitchen! Another good hiding place.

She crawled fast as she could, pushing the crutch ahead of her, and disappeared behind the counter. She opened all the lower cupboards first, and looked beneath the sink. No tanks! And nothing else in the least suspicious.

Didn't criminals sometimes hide things in flour tins and cookie jars? She rose from the floor, realizing nobody could see her here from outside. And there, on the wall panel at the end of the counter, prominently displayed, was her caricature of Mrs. Guizot! Framed, too, just as she'd said, with pretty dark green matting. Dash swallowed. It made her feel even more guilty.

But if Mrs. Guizot knew nothing about all this—if that man was using her— "Search!" Dash reminded herself. "Look for loot, treasure, anything!"

She searched in the higher cupboards—there were no flour tins or cookie jars. In fact there was very little in the way of food—just orderly rows of dishes and glasses, and a variety of spices. My, Mrs. Guizot was neat! There wasn't much in the refrigerator, either. Just fruit, cheese, and an unopened bottle of champagne.

Dash ducked down and hobbled on to the rear of the house where there were two bedrooms with a bathroom in between. She searched in the bathroom first, behind the shower curtain, under the small sink and in the cupboard, which held only another orderly row of suntan lotion, shampoo, and sundries. Remembering the movies, she even lifted the toilet tank! No small pouch dangling there with hidden jewels or something. . . .

Oh, if she only knew *what* she was looking for! Jewels? Gold coins? Some sort of "treasure"? Or drugs, microfilm secrets—any of those horrible possibilities JC had mentioned. That kind of thing was sometimes hidden in cold cream jars or toothpaste tubes! At least in the movies. But there were no cold cream jars in the bathroom! And—could she squeeze out a toothpaste tube? No! Someone would know the house had been searched.

Enough light from the living room spilled to the rear so she didn't need the flashlight. The doors to both bedrooms were standing open. At the door of the bathroom, Dash looked from one to the other. Which first? One looked unused, like a waiting guest room. The other was obviously Mrs. Guizot's. If he were hiding something from her, using the house, wouldn't it be clever to hide it right under her nose, where she'd never suspect it?

Dash limped into Mrs. Guizot's room first. She wasn't prepared for the mirror over the bureau. Hobbling toward it she gasped—seeing a strange looking creature. It looked like a ghost! But it was only herself, white-faced, stumbling forward on her crutch. Her heart pounded and it took a minute to recover.

Time was going on! Too much time. She hurried to look in the corners of the room, under the bed, in the closet . . . nothing but those gay print shifts Mrs. Guizot wore, sweaters, raincoat, robe, and shoes. Another straw hat on the shelf.

What had she missed? Her eyes swept the room, and she looked back at the bureau. A vase stood on it, with the weeds Mrs. Guizot wore in her hat, and below, of course, were all those drawers. . . . Oh, she couldn't snoop in those private things! It wasn't fair.

She rushed on to the other bedroom, glanced quickly around, under the bed, and then in that bureau. Clean as a whistle. There was nothing in any of the drawers. Well, of course there wouldn't be, she remembered. Mr. "Herrick" wasn't here now. There was only Dan Alexander—supposedly, up at the round house. And if he wanted to "pretend" to be Jason Herrick and return to get anything he might have left—

"Oh, poor Mrs. Guizot!" thought Dash. "She'll never know what's happened."

She blinked around the room, convinced she'd never find anything, but opened the closet door anyway. . . .

And had the fright of her life! She jumped so hard she almost fell down. He was *hanging* in there! Her skin crawled. She almost fainted. She got so dizzy everything blurred. And then came into focus.

He wasn't hanging there—the dark business suit was. But right above, on the closet shelf, was the black wig. And next to that a plastic bag—and on the closet floor, as she looked down, a pair of black shoes and a *briefcase*!

"Ohhh!" Dash shuddered while her heart pounded and a hundred things came to her mind at once.

With the wig right above the suit and the shoes directly beneath, it had looked like a *person* hanging in the closet. And it was! Mr. "Jason Herrick"—and Mrs. Guizot must know all about everything! So she wasn't an innocent victim—JC had been right all along. They were in cahoots about something. . . .

Chills raced up and down Dash's spine. She was scared to death. But she grabbed the briefcase and shook it. Nothing rattled; there was no sound, nothing inside. *Lining,* she thought frantically. Cut the lining—it could be hidden there. But then they'd know—unless she took it—no, they'd know even more. That it was missing! What to do? She took down the plastic bag and looked inside. The beard! And spirit gum! Should she take *that*? Sure proof of a disguise. . . .

What to do?

And suppose the loot wasn't hidden in the briefcase lining?

She was shaking from head to toe. Take the briefcase? Take the beard? They needed *proof* of something! She hadn't looked in Gizzard's bureau—

"And now she's Gizzard," Dash thought wildly. She didn't know what to do! Hastily, she shoved the plastic bag back on the shelf, replaced the briefcase, and stumbled on to Mrs. Guizot's room, to the bureau.

Hazily, she thought that if she didn't find anything, she'd go back and take the beard.

She opened the top drawer and a beautiful piece of jewelry winked up from an open tray. Dash stared. It was exquisite, unlike anything she'd ever seen before. It was surrounded by loops of shell beads and other familiar costume jewelry. She picked it up, amazed. Who would leave anything like this lying around in an open house—unless it was deliberately placed in the "open," as if it meant nothing?

It looked ancient, antique, and real. Like a real emerald pendant hanging from a long, intricately worked silver chain. She shivered. Could JC have been right about "pirate treasure"? This could be *it*! Or a part of it. But she didn't know enough about jewelry! Both her mother and Candy hated to wear it. . . .

But anyone seeing this would know it was something unusual. Should she take it? Was this their "proof"? Or go back for the beard? They needed *something*— but taking this would be stealing. Taking anything would be stealing! And they'd know someone had been here.

She heard voices from outside on the Bay Walk. Somebody was coming along. It could be Mrs. Guizot! She had to get out! She dropped the pendant back in the tray and shut the drawer. Her crutch was leaning against the bureau. She grabbed it, turned, and it struck the vase with the weeds. Dash lurched for it, but not in time. It rocked and crashed to the floor.

"Oh, no!" she gasped. It shattered beside the bureau and water ran over the floor.

Outside, the voices were closer and louder, and she

couldn't tell if it was Mrs. Guizot or not. She looked about, panicked, and saw a small balcony outside the bedroom windows, off a door. She hopped over—locked! But steps led down to the back of the house.

She slid back the latch and unlocked the door. Her hands were shaking. Trying to make no sound, she stepped out, closed the door behind her and hopped down the steps with her crutch.

The flashlight fell out of her sweatshirt pouch and rolled on the cement with a terrific clatter.

Dash froze, stock still, at the bottom of the steps, listening. The voices seemed only a few feet away. Then they sounded fainter, and she heard no sound from the house above.

It was pitch black down here behind the house. She sank to the cement and reached around, trying to find the flashlight. Her hand reached and groped—she couldn't feel it anywhere! Maybe it had rolled into the weeds separating the house from the one in back. Or it could have rolled in the other direction, under the house.

More voices—no, *a* voice! —a single voice humming, coming from the direction of the dock. A woman's hum!

Forget the flashlight! Dash plunged ahead, straight into the weeds, and then plowed through the garden around the next house, stumbling through shrubs and flower beds, across to the garden where they'd hidden the cot.

She fell across it, face first, and lay there, panting. First she felt hot, then cold as ice. Midges and mosquitos swarmed around her. Where was JC?

It seemed an awfully long time before she heard a movement, and then JC's voice whispering, "Dash?"

"Here," she gulped.

"I did it!" he hissed proudly. "I went in when she started dessert, and first it was *horrible*—then it wasn't so scary. Did you find anything? Did you see a tank?"

"No tank," she moaned, "but I sure found something! I lost something, too. Never mind—you were right all the time, JC. She's in on it. That's for sure!"

"How do you know?" he whispered eagerly. "What did you find?"

She grabbed his arm in the dark. "I found Mr. Jason Herrick!"

15

~~~~~~
~~~~~~

"YOU BROKE a vase?" said JC, aghast, a little while later. They sat in his room while Dash nervously drew the night's events in her calendar. "*And you unlocked the back door? And lost the flashlight?* Some Great Brain! Now she'll know someone sneaked in."

"I'm sorry," Dash swallowed. "I couldn't help it. But maybe she'll think a cat got in and knocked over the vase."

"What about the back *door*?" yelped JC.

"Well—" Dash cast about for any hopeful thought. "Maybe she'll forget it was locked! The front door was open. Maybe she forgot to lock it. Maybe she's forgetful."

"Maybe, maybe everything," groaned JC. "And what if she finds a strange flashlight under the house?"

"Oh—oh," said Dash, rattled, "anybody could lose a flashlight. Anybody!"

"Yeah, right under a house with a broken vase and an unlocked door!" He shuddered. "Long as you did all that you might as well have taken something! The wig—the beard—the necklace! Especially the necklace. Then she might think it was an ordinary burglar."

"Maybe she still will think so," whispered Dash.

"*Her*?" He shuddered again. "Not her! She's slick. What burglar would go in there and not steal the necklace? Huh? Does that make sense? I'll bet she left it for bait, so, if anybody did snoop around, they'd take it quick, and not look for the rest of the loot."

"Oh, JC, I looked—and looked."

"You didn't look in every book!"

"I couldn't!" wailed Dash. "There wasn't time."

"Did you look for a wall safe? You know, like hidden behind a picture or something?"

Dash stared at him. "I didn't think of that."

He struck his head. "And *me,* giving her back that twenty dollars. Oh, boy, is she going to know something's fishy!"

"How did she act at the restaurant?" asked Dash. "What happened?" So far they'd only talked about her part of things.

"Weird!" JC rolled up his eyes. "Fluttering, crazy,

very happy to see me! Then she got furious about the money, and argued—just like you said. Then she got very sweet and smiling, but she still wouldn't take it. And she talked about you, on and on—"

"What did she say?" asked Dash nervously.

"Let's see—well, first I said what you told me to, that you couldn't accept so much for a little cartoon sketch. Then she got very strange." JC imitated Mrs. Guizot and her voice, " 'It is *not* a cartoon, and *not* a little sketch! All of Darcy's drawings are the first works of a gifted child who is destined to become a *great* artiste! They are all *important* drawings!' "

"Was she kidding?" asked Dash. "Or serious?"

JC frowned. "I couldn't tell. She wasn't exactly kidding, but I don't know how serious she was, either. Oh, wow, she's something!"

"What happened about the money?"

"I left it," he said. "I told her you would have given it back yourself, but you'd hurt your leg again and had to stay quiet. But you insisted. Then I just put it on the table and scrammed."

"Did she believe you—about my leg?" whispered Dash.

He shrugged. "I guess so. She didn't say anything. But listen, you've got to keep it up now! You've got to wear that bandage every day. Pretend you're in pain and everything. Otherwise she'll think giving back the money was suspicious, with you not there—"

"She's bound to tell *him* about the broken vase, too," added Dash apprehensively.

"Right! So you've got to stay out on deck in the cot, and not walk at all! Make sure he gets a good look at you."

"JC, maybe we should tell somebody now! I found the disguise—it's there."

"It won't be there now," he shook his head at her wildly. "She'll pack it away, the minute she sees that vase. And he's hidden the tanks somewhere—nobody'd find them. And you didn't find the loot!"

"I could show this—" She waved the cartoon calendar at him.

"That!" he sniffed. "Who'd believe it? It's good, but it looks like you're inventing some new comic book. *The Littlewood Kids: Detectives.*"

He was in that ancient, solemn, gnomelike mood, Dash saw. His eyes were round and unblinking, as if he looked at invisible, faraway things.

"And what do you plan to do, JC?" Dash asked him suspiciously.

"Huh?" He returned to her with a start. "Oh, me, I'll be a crazy kid again. You know, a cut-up. Real stupid and cheerful. Fly my kite, run around, yell a lot—if some more kids come out, maybe I'll play with them."

"And leave me alone on the deck?" she cried.

"Oh, I'll be in and out," he grinned.

"JC!" Dash suddenly remembered. "Daddy's coming on the fifth! That's Tuesday. What's he going to say if he sees me in this?" She looked at the bandaged leg. "How long do you think I'll have to pretend?"

"Until everything's over," he said matter-of-factly.

And that meant, thought Dash, that she'd have a heck of a time explaining it to her mother and Candy.

She hid the calendar under JC's mattress, wondering what in the world they could do to prove any of this to anyone. If only they weren't "The Littlewood Kids"! If only JC wasn't going to be The World's Greatest Actor, and she The World's Greatest Cartoonist. Sometimes, being "gifted" like this could really boomerang!

However, things seemed to be "over" sooner than they expected. Dash had to spend just one day, Thursday, lying on the cot on deck, with her leg prominently up and out in the bandage. Candy narrowed her eyes at it suspiciously but didn't say a word. Audrey said only, and very quietly, "If you were fibbing to me about hurting it, Dash, I'm going to be very angry."

JC cavorted all day on the deck, the beach, the walk, the dune steps. His antics seemed to no avail, and like a most unnecessary production, for Dan Alexander didn't appear until late afternoon, walking up from the bay with his surfboard.

To make sure he saw her in the bandaged leg, Dash waved and yelled, "Hi!"

She got a brief wave in return before he walked into the round house. And on his next somersault across the deck, JC hissed, "Pretend you're in pain."

So Dash groaned loudly, and JC directed, "Not so loud! You're overacting." He righted himself, bent solicitously over the cot, gave the leg a brief pat, and sat cross-legged beside her on the deck, as if he were cheering a patient.

They played cards, stayed out on the porch that evening where Dan Alexander could see them—if he were looking—and Dash made a great business of limping with her crutch when she finally went off to bed. The man hadn't gone out to surf all day or evening.

And then on Friday he left.

They were at the dock, which seemed the logical

place to be, as everyone else was there watching the new arrivals.

The first of July! The dock and the walks were crowded with people moving in for the season. Trains of little wagons stuffed with luggage and cartons of food, and sometimes children and dogs, moved inland from the dock. The freight boat had carried bicycles, playpens, surfboards, odds and ends of furniture like extra deck and rocking chairs. People milled about the freight house, collecting their larger items on dollies which they wheeled away. This was the busiest weekend so far, with many visitors as well as renters and homeowners. The Fourth of July weekend was always the biggest, until Labor Day.

JC had parked the cot against the dock rail, away from the crush of people. One ferry after another discharged its passengers and left.

At the very last moment, just before a ferry pulled away, Dan Alexander tore down the dock, bumping into people, and leaped aboard. It was him, himself, with his blonde hair, dressed in slacks and a sports shirt! No Jason Herrick disguise! He was carrying a regular-sized suitcase in his hand.

"There goes the loot!" said JC disgustedly. "Now there'll never be another chance."

"Let's go home," sighed Dash.

JC could hardly maneuver the cot around the crowds, but finally they broke free and headed toward the ocean, surrounded by wagons, bicycles, tricycles, children, and dogs.

"Unless," said JC, "he might have left something in the round house—"

"Oh, he wouldn't take the chance," said Dash. "They know somebody was in The Lookout—that's why he didn't wear the Herrick disguise. No, whatever he had, I'll bet he took it *all* with him. They've probably buried the suit and the wig and the beard—"

"Or dumped it in the Great South Bay," said JC gloomily.

"I wonder who they think got in there?" said Dash with a little shiver.

"Not you!" JC wheeled the cot up the ramp to their deck and patted her leg. "Good old leg! I think we should frame the bandage."

Dash looked at him with surprise. "But you were so worried! What makes you think now they don't suspect us?"

"Because if they did, they'd have done something about it. Old Gazebo would have come nosing around—or something."

"Hm," murmured Dash, wondering, as she limped into the porch.

"But there's nothing worse in the whole world than having a real mystery and not being able to prove it!" said JC. He flopped on the couch and shook his fist at the round house.

"Much less solve it!" Dash agreed. It made her angry, too. They'd learned so much, just to have it fizzle out like this. They knew he'd been in disguise. They knew where the disguise had been kept. They knew Mrs. Guizot was involved. Somehow! Dash still hoped that she was involved in a sort of innocent way. She could be. . . .They knew about the false scuba tanks, and that he surfed out to get something. They were even pretty sure where he got them from—but not to know what was *in* them—

"It's horrible!" said Dash. "That jewelry could be part of it, but we're not sure."

"We probably never will be," said JC heavily.

"I wonder if he'll ever come back?" Dash mused, looking at the round house.

"Sure he will. He's not renting this summer, remember?"

"Well, even if he does," sighed Dash, "even if he surfs all summer, it's still over. I guess we were lousy detectives."

"Yeah, Great Falcon," said JC with a sour face.

"And Great, really Great Elephant Brain!" sniffed Dash.

They both felt dismal for the rest of the day, and all day Saturday, too.

16

ON SUNDAY afternoon Dash sat on the porch with a sketch pad on her knee, looking out the screen door. The noise, activity, and voices all around made it seem almost like Coney Island. She had never seen so many people on the beach.

She didn't care about *not* drawing anymore; it was something to keep her eyes and hands busy. At least when she drew, which she had all day Saturday, too, she wasn't plagued with their unsolved mystery. If she wasn't occupied with drawing, she thought of it constantly and it drove her wild!

She was trying to draw the distant beach scene through the screen door, using it as a "frame," and was doing it terribly. JC, in swim trunks and a shirt, looked with longing at the crowded beach.

"Go on out," said Dash. "I'm just going to sit here and fiddle anyway."

"Sure? You won't be lonesome?"

"Nope. And if I am, it's my fault, anyway."

JC grabbed his red kite from a corner. "If you want to do me, I'll fly it front of the house."

"No, thanks, JC. Go meet some kids and have fun. You can introduce me later."

The door banged behind him as he ran out.

There were lots of kites sailing high in the sky, glinting red, gold, and silver in the sun. It was a wonderful kite-flying, clothes-drying day. All along the walk, beside and behind the houses, sheets and towels snapped in the wind. People walked by the porch every few minutes, going back and forth from the beach. The volleyball net was set up below and shouts from the players carried up to the house.

Nobody else was home. Candy was out with Eric and a new group of young people on his boat. Audrey had taken a long, long walk, all the way to the lighthouse, hoping to escape the crowds. She couldn't wait for the Fourth to end, and for Tuesday. Dash wasn't nearly so excited about her father's arrival now. She had really looked forward to greeting him with a "Hi! Guess what happened!" And then to telling him what clever little sleuths they had been.

Wind from the open windows tickled the back of her neck and rustled the pages of the art pad. She looked down and scratched out the last drawing. It was dreadful! All of her drawings yesterday and today had been dreadful.

She had tried to shade instead of being so "linear" as Mr. Hildebrand said, tried to see in and around and in back of things. Hildy was always talking about seeing, how to see, learning to see, seeing more and more. Oh, he was strange and kind of wonderful, thought Dash with a twinge of guilt again.

He was so different from her first art teacher who thought the answer to everything lay in drawing and yet more drawing. Not Hildy! He'd turned the whole class upside down, wanting them to work with different materials, wood, clay, metal—even finger paint!

"Get messy!" he'd roared. "Dig in, experiment. Learn to see with your hands, your toes, the back of your heads. It's all in how you see."

He'd brought a microscope into class those first days, she remembered, and cut sections of nuts, berries, flowers, leaves, showing them the precise unfolding patterns in the world of tiny things. Then he took them to the planetarium to see the vast worlds of the universe. . . .

Dash would never forget the first time she showed him her stack of drawings, two years' worth of sketches, and confided her ambition to become the Greatest Cartoonist in the World. She had thought he would scoff, but he didn't.

He'd said, "There aren't many great female cartoonists. We could use some more. We need the view." But then he demanded, "*Why* do you want to become a cartoonist?"

And Dash had tried her best to explain; how she

didn't think cartoons were silly; how she seemed to see the world and people in a slightly exaggerated way; how she loved to catch movements and expressions.

She remembered struggling for words. "Because cartoons can show what's behind things."

And Hildy had stared so hard it made her uncomfortable. "It's good that you're a serious person. Only serious people can be good cartoonists. You're right. Great cartoons uncover the absurdity of things. They can help the world."

Dash had shivered, absolutely dazzled by this remark. He'd gone on to explain that the word "cartoon" originally meant the preliminary sketches that great artists like Rafael and Michaelangelo drew, prior to actually painting. That had certainly made her think! And then he'd cautioned her about too much drawing, pointing out the dangers of getting set in a style. "Learn to *see*," was Hildy's refrain.

Well, thought Dash, she'd tried, at least yesterday and today, even if she'd tried through drawing. She thought if she could see more, she might be able to "see" what was in those tanks! So far she sure hadn't "helped the world!"

She'd drawn the backs of people instead of their faces, sea gulls flying away, the inside of shells, as far as she could peer into them, from Audrey's vast collection. She'd drawn the pebbles and stones her mother brought in, trying to imagine how they looked deep inside. She'd even sent JC to the store for water colors, and tried to catch another mystery—the sea. It emerged limpid, washed out, with no life or sparkle at all, and no feeling whatever of depth.

"I'm not and never will be any good at this at all," she thought aloud. "I'll just have to go on doing lines, and more lines."

The only good thing she'd done, in fact, was her cartoon calendar of events! Dash began to wonder if she ever saw anything at all other than in quick sketches and caricatures? She'd seen that pointed elbow all right, and the expression of Mrs. Guizot's face. She saw the way they both moved and walked—but did she really see *them*?

Dash threw her pencil across the porch and tossed the art pad aside. What was she sitting here brooding for? She looked across the walk to the round house. There was no way inside now to look for any scraps of evidence. And most likely there weren't any!

She looked out at the beach, at the windy, sunny, exciting day. Let Candy or her mother kill her! She was going, by gosh, to the *beach*. She hopped up, grabbed a driftwood stick Audrey had collected, and went out the door.

Down the ramp, up and down the dune steps, to the deep, purple-colored sand that felt warm under her feet. Oh, it was wonderful! Dash stood for a moment, looking, smelling. The sun sparkled, the water sparkled, white caps blew in the wind, the air smelled deliciously of salt. People were everywhere, lying on the sand, sitting under umbrellas, walking along the shoreline. Children and dogs scampered in and out of the waves. The lifeguard was perched on his high platform, watching swimmers and a family in a small rubber boat that was bouncing in on the waves. Besides salt, there was a trace of suntan lotion in the air.

The soles of her feet grew hot, and Dash plowed

ahead, finding it difficult to move through the deep sand. But then it changed, becoming firmer and lighter in color, until finally it felt cold and hard and damp under her feet—and then heaven! Her toes were in the ocean and surf boomed and crashed loudly in her ears.

A wave broke, rushed in, and covered her with foam. Dash sank down, rooted to her ankles. Another huge breaker crashed, slapping her with spray. A tide of water knocked her backward and she went down flat on her bottom, covered with wet sand and ocean.

"Oh, sea!" she yelled when the water rushed out again. "Beautiful wonderful sea!" She sat there licking the salt on her lips, letting the waves run in and drench her. Wet, wet, wet! She'd never been so happy!

A beautiful young German shepherd splashed through the water and playfully snatched her piece of driftwood in his mouth. He stood, wagging his tail, then ran off with it and stopped to look back at her. It was an invitation.

"Come on," cried Dash, and he zoomed back, dropping it in her lap. She tossed it out to the waves, and he happily plunged in, swimming out to retrieve it. They played the game over and over, until one of the incoming waves brought in a jellyfish and left it stranded right beside Dash.

The dog ran off, barking, and Dash stood up with her stick to look at it. Her mother had never added one of these to her collection! But it was fascinating. A large round transparent glob with masses of evil-looking red stuff in the center. The next wave brought in a lot of them, and the swimmers began leaving the sea. Dash moved away, too, so she wouldn't get stung.

She walked along the beach above the waterline, gazing down at the pebbles and seashells. While they were still wet like this, they looked like a collection of jewels. There were dark blue oyster "slippers," large white clam shells, tiny fan-shaped ones of orange and black. Pebbles and small stones gleamed with color; pink, purple, yellow, bright orange, green, milky white. No wonder Audrey was a scavenger!

Children and dogs ran past her, but Dash paid no attention. She was glued to the fascination of the beach. Strands of dark brown seaweed, a sea anemone, the opaque white and deep black pebbles people used in gardens—a lovely piece of sand glass! Her mother loved these small pieces of blue and green glass that had been rolled and polished by the ocean until they were as smooth as silk.

She dropped her stick and leaned over to pick it up. When she rose, Dan Alexander was standing still, not five feet away, staring at her!

Her heart thudded, but she tried to smile.

His expression didn't change. He looked her hard in the eyes, and then gazed directly down at her legs. The look seemed to take forever. Dash couldn't breathe. She was frozen with that silly smile.

He shifted his eyes then and looked past her, but still didn't move. His face was grim, as if he were deciding something. Then, with no smile, and no "Hello," he strode silently past her.

The sunny, busy beach, suddenly shifted and blurred. Dizzily, Dash sank to the sand before she fell down. Her head pounded. She didn't dare look back at him. That stare of his was the most threatening experience of her life! Even seeing the disguise in the closet hadn't frightened her as much as this.

She was so scared she couldn't see well. It was as if dark clouds had moved in on the beach. She put her head down, remembering that's what people who were going to faint were supposed to do.

She looked at her leg. Round, tan, firm—*why* hadn't she thought of wearing that bandage! How stupid could anyone be! He could have been watching her walk along for some time. Of course, she'd had the stick—her thoughts whirled.

It was Sunday. He'd seen her lying in the cot, in "pain" on Thursday, and probably Friday, before he left on the ferry. Could she have "healed" in just one day and a half? After that big production? Oh, it was one thing to be seen on the beach, but she hadn't been really limping along—and nobody who'd hurt a leg again would go out without support! At least a good, bracing bandage, if not crutches. But nobody who'd hurt an already broken leg again would even *try* the beach so soon!

Of course he'd know she'd been "staging" the hurt leg. He'd guess that she could have been the "burglar" in The Lookout . . . but why would that matter now?

Dash stared out at the ocean, not seeing it. It was just a blue mass, heaving and swaying like her thoughts.

If everything was over, as they thought, why would he even care about her leg? Why would he care if she had sneaked into Mrs. Guizot's house—even found the disguise? Whatever he knew or suspected, it was obvious that she and JC hadn't done a thing about it! Obviously, they hadn't spilled the beans! Didn't he know that they couldn't prove anything?

But that look of his! She shivered, feeling weak and dizzy again. It was the worst look she'd ever received in her life. It was like a message, a warning—

Of course! It *was* a warning. He might as well have said it aloud: "I know what you and your brother are up to, and you'd better not say a word. Or else—!"

That was it! And also, maybe she'd been wrong. Maybe he *was* going to surf out again and bring in more tanks! But the message was clear. "Watch out."

And maybe—Dash's heart started to pound again—maybe he thought they *had* discovered what he was bringing in! Had she missed it? Had she seen it, and not known it? What had she seen and skipped over in Mrs. Guizot's house?

She got up and stumbled in from the beach, heading home by a different walk. She was icy cold and shaking. Where had he come from? He'd been wearing the same outfit he had when he left, but walking from the direction of Ocean Beach. No suitcase—of course!

She crossed through the sand in back of the houses on the other walk, and went home by the back door. Their sheets were billowing from the clothes line by the shower. Dash felt chilled all through.

JC found her taking a hot shower, and pounded on the door of the wooden shed.

"He's home! He's back! He went out surfing again and left his front door wide open. Hey—come out of there, Dash! This time you can keep him busy talking when he comes back. It's my turn to go and snoop."

She turned off the faucets, wrapped herself in her terry cloth robe, and came out looking as white as the sheets behind JC's head.

"It's no good," she trembled. "He saw me—he knows everything. If that door is wide open, JC, it's a trap!"

She told him all about what had happened on the beach, and JC looked appropriately impressed. But not quite as impressed, meaning not as scared, as she was.

And that night Dash had a new scare about JC's attitude toward all this. She was sitting on his bunk bed, drawing what she hoped were the last cartoons for her calendar. The very last was a sketch of the round house with the door wide open, and an empty tank inside with a question mark balloon.

"An invitation to disaster," she pointed out.

But JC, sitting beside her, scrunched himself back against the wall, hugged his knees and closed his eyes. He smiled in a canary-swallowing manner.

"You're not getting any ideas, are you, JC?" She looked at him suspiciously. "Listen, that look was no joke! That man is no joke! You can't go into the round house. Even if he leaves the door open again."

JC just smiled and she stared at him.

"Didn't you say you were a coward? Well, this is the time to *be* one! Don't you dare go into that house. Promise me you won't try. Solemn promise!"

"Okay, I'm a coward and I won't go in," he said.

Dash looked at his hands. No crossed fingers. She looked at his toes, scabby and spread out. No crossed toes.

"Okay," she sighed, accepting his oath, and wrote her signature by the last cartoon. *Dash.*

Below she printed: *End of the unsolved mystery, July 3, Fire Island.*

17

~~~~~~
~~~~~~

MONDAY, THE Fourth of July, arrived in the weirdest way. Early in the morning the island was blanketed by a low mist. By noon it had become a thick fog. By late afternoon everything was black as night, and hidden in what one usually thought of as a London pea-souper, only worse. Yesterday's wind still prevailed and was blowing in hard from the sea, while along the beach, people were setting off firecrackers. They flew back inland, snatched and carried by the wind. Streaks of red sailed through the fog, landing on dune grass, boardwalks, the wooden decks and roofs of oceanfront houses.

Audrey was enraged. All afternoon she had stood on the deck, watching with a flashlight and a hose in her hand, ready to drown any fire that began. Nothing could be more dangerous than these sizzling firecrackers in the wind.

"Where do they get them?" she kept saying. "And who's setting them off?"

Candy was standing by to help. "Probably kids who don't know what they're doing. And they must have brought them out from the city. They couldn't buy them here."

A supervised display of fireworks was scheduled for the beach that night. "But they won't have it," Audrey said. "It's too dangerous."

"They will if the wind falls," said Candy. "The Fire Department runs it, and I heard someone say it's safer to have it and satisfy the kids than have this go on all night."

They'd heard the fire siren twice. And Mrs. Morris, the real estate agent, had phoned to make sure someone was home to watch the house.

It was the strangest day-night Dash had ever experienced. In fact there was no difference between day and night. She couldn't see more than a few inches ahead. Everyone was out on deck, but she knew where they were only by their flashlights. She heard laughter in the darkness. People from the house behind them seemed to be having a party. In spite of the fog there was a gay, holiday mood, which made things even eerier. Others were stumbling up and down the walk happily shouting that it was the end of the world!

Two people had come up to their deck, completely lost. The only sign of their presence was the vibration of their feet and the beam of their flashlights shining through the fog.

"Is this Kismet?" they'd asked.

"Oh, heavens, no!" said Audrey. "You're in Fair Harbor."

They'd all laughed, but really it wasn't funny. The couple had walked all the way from Ocean Beach on their way to friends in Kismet. They were very tired, and if they ever did reach Kismet, they'd never get back tonight. A strange Fourth of July!

All day long JC had been crazy. Slinking through the house, hiding, walking on cat feet, jumping out to scare everyone, until finally Audrey told him to stop. He loved the day! And he didn't completely stop. He waved his flashlight in crazy circles, making patterns in the dark, and kept hissing, "Ah, what a night for Mandarin Falcon!"

He worried Dash terribly. She was afraid he was working himself up to sneaking into the round house, even though he'd promised not to. There was something suspicious about that promise, she felt. She tried to keep track of him by the waving beam of his tiny light on the deck. Audrey had the large flashlight, Candy a smaller one, and JC was using a small penlight.

Dash, of course, didn't have a flashlight at all now. Audrey was too worried about possible fires to even be angry that she'd lost it. She simply told Dash to sit in a deck chair, watch, and not move.

A red streak flew through the air, landed somewhere in front of the deck and exploded with a loud bang. Dash jumped. "JC?" she called. He should go down below the house to check on it.

There was no answer, but his light was still there, waist high and steady.

"JC?" she whispered again. She got up from her chair and stumbled across to the beam of light, feeling around. No JC! But his light fell from the arm of a deck chair. He'd left it!

Dash was furious, and then scared. Nobody could walk off anywhere in this fog without a light. Unless—she looked in the direction of the round house. It was impossible to even see if lights were on. But he had *promised*, anyway. JC never broke his promises unless he crossed his fingers or toes. . . . His *eyes*! Dash suddenly remembered his eyes had been closed. Crossed eyes?

She picked up the small penlight and moved quietly across the deck. She heard water spurting from the hose. Audrey was spraying the deck and the dune grass out front just to make sure. She turned off the light and felt her way to the ramp, hanging to the rail as she went down.

On the walk she turned on the light again, but still couldn't see very much ahead. She almost had to guess where the other ramp led to the round house, and then groped her way up to the lower deck.

"JC?" she whispered softly. No answer. She looked

up. The fog was like thick brown soup, but from here she should be able to see if a light was on. Everything looked dark. Something jumped at her in the tiny beam of her light—just the edge of the surfboard, she saw with relief! It was propped up against the door. . . .

The *open* door! Trap, trap, trap! And JC had probably walked right into it! Oh, why didn't he understand that it could really be dangerous? Why couldn't he be a coward again! Ever since he'd been brave enough to speak to Mrs. Guizot in the restaurant, JC had somehow changed. Dash had the feeling he thought he could do anything! And suppose that fellow was lurking inside, just waiting for him—or her?

She tried to think, and all she could think of was the terrible look he'd given her on the beach. The warning, "Back off! Stay out of this!"

Well, if JC was here, she thought nervously, the only way to find him and get him *out*, was by acting as natural as she could. She swallowed, then pounded on the doorjamb, calling inside loudly, "Hello? Mr. Alexander? Are you there?"

No answer. No sound of movement within.

She tried again, "We've lost my brother—have you seen him? My mother sent him over to borrow a flashlight. . . . Hello?"

There wasn't a sound. Fog swirled around her and in the open door. She was terrified to go inside, but she had to find JC! He would have heard her calling if he were outside, near or underneath the house. Once more she called loudly, "JC—are you in there?"

The house was as dark and silent as a tomb. Could JC possibly be hiding from *her*? He'd been so crazy all day. And maybe—could Mr. Alexander possibly have just stepped out, going over to the party in the other house? Dash tried to reassure herself with ideas before she finally stepped inside the house.

Her tiny light showed an open area downstairs, with four doors around a central, circular staircase. She opened each door into the small, pie-shaped bedrooms, calling "JC?" And then climbed up the stairs, saying, "JC, if you're in here, come out! Answer me!"

At the head of the stairs she stopped and swept the light around. The beam was too tiny to disclose things clearly, and she stumbled, groping around the furniture, looking in back of the couch and chairs. No JC!

She advanced on the large bar counter that took up one side of the room. It was behind this that they'd seen the fallen, phony scuba tank. It'd be just like JC to hide here! The house felt so empty that Dash was now convinced Dan Alexander wasn't home. And she really expected JC to jump up from behind that counter, and scare her.

But nothing of the sort happened. And when she looked behind it, JC wasn't there. But there was a sink, with a high, wide cupboard space beneath, just the size for Mandarin Falcon. She sat on the floor and opened the cupboard doors. Nothing! No Great Falcon. Just cleansers and soap and scrubbing brushes—and behind them, a gray cylinder lying on its side. . . .

Dash stared at it, not breathing. It couldn't be! She played her light over the surface. It was! A tank, just like the one they'd seen. Oh, she couldn't let this opportunity slip by! She put the penlight on the floor beside her, shoved the cleaning stuff aside, and dragged it out.

A phony scuba tank! She saw the seam where it fitted together. It must unscrew somehow! She tried to get it open, but the metal was slippery and difficult to manage. She put it between her knees, got a grip, and finally it began to turn.

"I shouldn't be doing this," Dash thought apprehensively. "I'm crazy! I should get out of here. And maybe JC just went to the beach—"

But she couldn't resist! Of course there wouldn't be anything inside now—but maybe just a tiny scrap of something? A little clue? At least she could see how it was made! Watertight, of course; she saw that instantly when the two halves came apart. She shone her light into one half—it was empty. But in the other—she didn't believe it!—was something wrapped in a sort of plastic.

She pulled it out, trembling. This was impossible! She couldn't have found anything! It was loosely rolled up, like a scroll. It spread apart easily, and Dash laid it on the floor beside her light. She carefully lifted the plastic covering and there, underneath, was one of the most beautiful paintings she had ever seen.

Art! Of course!

Not drugs or secret microfilms or any of the things they had guessed. Stolen masterpieces! Or forgeries? Mrs. Guizot! That was her connection with all this. She knew about art—her husband, her father—oh! Dash sucked in her breath. It was all coming clear.

A door banged, a light went on, and a voice chirped, "Well! Did you finally find what you've been looking for, Darcy-Dash?"

13

DASH JUMPED so hard the tank rolled with a terrific clatter.

Mrs. Guizot's face, framed in a dark green hood, twinkled down at her over the counter. "Come on out now," she wagged a finger playfully. "Give me the canvas."

Slowly, Dash pulled herself up and handed Mrs. Guizot the painting.

"It was my idea!" Mrs. Guizot sang out gaily. "I put it there just for you to find. What a shame for you to go to all that trouble and not have the joy of discovery! Wasn't it fun?"

She walked to the couch, placed the painting on the coffee table, and beckoned to Dash. "And isn't this the perfect night for this sort of thing! My word, the fog was made to order!"

Dash was still so stunned she couldn't speak. Mrs. Guizot, acting so bright and gay, looked like a strange monk or a crazy wizard. The green hood was part of a long pullover, tied around her waist with gold cord. It had a small gold tassel on the pointed peak. Underneath she wore slacks and sneakers, and looked as if she were dressed for some part in a play.

"Come along," said Mrs. Guizot, patting the couch beside her. Slowly, Dash walked to her. "I know you wonder where I came from—through that door." She pointed to the upstairs door leading out to the top deck. "I've been waiting for you Darcy-Dash," she laughed. "I was sure you'd come, you or little Coleslaw."

"Where—uh—where is he?" Dash finally found her voice.

"Oh, I don't know, my dear, but I'm sure he'll turn up."

It was a strange answer, and Dash had an impulse to run out quickly, but Mrs. Guizot reached for her hand and pulled her down to the couch. "Don't go, Darcy. I'm sure you want to know all about this, and I'm going to tell you everything."

Dash hesitated on the edge of the couch. Did Mrs. Guizot know where JC was? And where was Dan Alexander? She made a movement, but Mrs. Guizot gripped her hand, and pouted at her.

"It wasn't very nice of you to pretend you'd hurt your leg again, Darcy. That was naughty!"

"But, I—"

"Oh, we know you can walk quite well! We've known since yesterday, when my friend saw you on the beach. And, of course, we suspected before that. We know you entered my house and broke the vase—don't deny it, Darcy!" Mrs. Guizot twinkled again. "It proves how very clever you are. Oh, my, children can be so clever!"

Dash didn't know what to say to that.

"I arranged all this, Darcy, just to show you something. I want us to share this together. Now—look. Just quietly take your time and look." Mrs. Guizot leaned forward, put her chin in her hands and stared dreamily at the painting on the table. "What do you think of it, Darcy-Dash?"

The light Mrs. Guizot had switched on was bright and illuminated the painting well. Dash looked—and looked again in wonder. She'd seen that it was beautiful, but it was even more; strange, hauntingly lovely. A land-scape with a farmhouse on a small hill. In the foreground were trees, a country lane, a dirt path leading to the house. In back were fields and streams, and yet beyond, more hills gently rising. Mountains rose in the distance, fold upon fold, with faraway peaks piercing the clouds. And above the clouds, a vast, infinite sky. . . .

As she really looked at it, Dash seemed to go into it. It wasn't like seeing a painting, it was like being there, walking down the lane, then up the path, and on and on. . . . She became lost in it, forgetting even where she was and who was with her.

"My father's work," said Mrs. Guizot softly. "I told you about him, but now you see. He had a very special gift for conveying vast spaces on small canvases."

Dash hadn't even noticed how small the canvas was. But Mrs. Guizot was right. It was incredible to see and feel and almost smell a whole other world within such small margins.

She shivered with awe. "It's—it's about the most wonderful thing I ever saw," she said sincerely.

"I knew you'd appreciate it," Mrs. Guizot smiled. "I wanted you to see at least one of these, and I'm sorry you couldn't see more. They're what we've been 'smuggling' in, you see!" She laughed. "I imagine you thought it was something far worse."

"Your father's own paintings!" cried Dash, wonderfully relieved. Everything was all right, then! But she remembered, "I thought—you said he gave them all away!"

"Oh, he did, my dear, he certainly did!" Mrs. Guizot still smiled, but differently. It was a scary smile. Her face was pinched and her voice tight. "First he gave all of his work away to friends, and then, before he died, to a museum in France. A *museum*! Gifts to the world. He left nothing to me, his daughter! Would you like to have a father who left you nothing?"

"I—I guess not," whispered Dash.

"He didn't even sign his work in the beginning! He thought *who* painted anything was unimportant. Only the work was important. Only as *gifts*. I told you he didn't realize how brilliant he was. Later, when he was recognized, his paintings became very valuable, and he was asked to sign them." Mrs. Guizot pointed to an almost invisible signature in the lower right corner of the painting.

"Roger Prudhomme," Mrs. Guizot sighed. "You

watch for that name, Darcy. You'll be hearing of it more and more."

Dash frowned, confused. "But—if he gave all his work away to friends and a museum—?"

"Oh, we stole them, my dear!" said Mrs. Guizot cheerfully. "Not from the friends; we'd never have been able to trace all of them. But he had sixteen oils in the museum, and I have all of those now. This is one."

"From the museum!" Dash was wide-eyed.

"Yes!" Mrs. Guizot rose with the painting and skimmed across the room to the counter where she carefully laid it down. She looked back at Dash, cocking her head. "I promised to tell you everything, and I will. But you must give me a promise in return—to tell me everything, too! Well?"

Slowly, Dash nodded. She didn't know what else to do! Could she get up and just leave? But where was JC! Mrs. Guizot was behaving as if all of this, the stolen paintings, scuba tanks, was just a little tea party. Maybe in her mind, it was! After all, they were her own father's work. . . .

"I was naughty, too," Mrs. Guizot giggled, walking back to the couch. "I shouldn't condemn you, Darcy-Dash. I pretended, too, that I had a 'late' husband. Well, he hasn't departed this world yet, my dear, he's very much alive! And bless his heart, he's assisted me in everything. He stole the paintings for me."

Dash was really scared now. Mrs. Guizot was telling her far too much, wasn't she?

"We spent two years planning this, and had the tanks specially designed in Europe. Watertight, of course, so the canvases would be perfectly safe. I'd been lucky enough to meet Mr. Alexander out here, who was willing to surf out and bring them in. Wasn't it a beautiful plan?"

Dash's heart was thudding, but she tried not to let Mrs. Guizot know how frightened she was. *Why* was the woman telling her all this?

"One thing I must know, Darcy," Mrs. Guizot suddenly grabbed her arm. "Did you and Coleslaw ever discover where my friend Dan got those tanks?"

"Ocean," Dash gulped automatically.

"Naturally. But do you know how? From where?"

Should she say anything at all, Dash wondered? But in a way it was obvious. "From a boat."

"Do you know which boat? *Which boat?*" Mrs. Guizot's hand tightened on her arm.

"Uh—uh, maybe a yacht?" squeaked Dash.

"Oh, what clever children!" Mrs. Guizot laughed. "You noticed the lovely yacht! You didn't miss anything, did you? Well, my dear, the yacht belongs to a friend of my husband; and it was so easy for him to suggest sailing off the coast of Fire Island. Well," she smiled at Dash encouragingly, "now that you know everything, you must tell me all—"

The upstairs door opened and Dan Alexander walked in, looking angry. "Haven't you had your fun, Blanche?"

"Oh, Dan, you must meet my little friend, Darcy Littlewood. I doubt if you've been properly introduced yet."

"We've met." He stared at Dash with the same grim look he'd given her yesterday.

It made her limp with fear. Why hadn't she run out

of here when she could?

"I was just telling Darcy all about the paintings and the yacht—"

"You're going to tell these kids everything?" he cried.

"Why not? They know nearly all of it already. The little children have found us out, Dan! They might as well have the satisfaction—"

"Ohh!" He made an impatient gesture and went out the door.

He had looked so menacing! Handsome, too, with the long blond hair and strong, muscular body. But that look had again scared Dash into a sort of paralysis. And he'd said *Kids*, not speaking of just one. . . . *Where was JC?*

Mrs. Guizot was sitting very straight on the couch, patting her hands on her knees like a child, smiling with satisfaction. She did look crazy, as JC thought she was, as she repeated to herself, "Oh, what a beautiful plan."

Dash thought she'd better run for it—now. She judged the distance from the couch to the stairwell, and looked at the upstairs door where Dan Alexander had gone out.

She was about to sprint when the door opened again and in came Dan Alexander, pulling JC behind him.

JC was tied! His feet hobbled, his arms twisted behind his back and caught with a clothes line! A large white handkerchief had fallen to his neck. He'd been muffled!

"Hi!" JC tried to smile at her.

19

~~~~~~~~~~~~~~~~~~~~~~~~~~~~~~
~~~~~~~~~~~~~~~~~~~~~~~~~~~~~~

DASH LEAPT from the couch, but Mrs. Guizot gripped her with a strong hand. And Dan Alexander made a threatening move at JC while he stared at Dash.

"One move from you," he said quietly, "and it won't be pleasant for your brother."

"Oh, Dan, do be gentle!" cried Mrs. Guizot. "They're only children. Now, everyone sit down and let's finish this. We haven't much time, and I must know a few things."

He shoved JC down in a chair and stood right beside him, keeping his eyes grimly on Dash. JC kept trying to smile, bravely, but his grin was frozen. All of his upper braces showed. He was so stiff that his toes stuck up and out, not moving an inch. He hardly breathed.

Dash shuddered and Mrs. Guizot patted her hand, "Oh, now don't be frightened, Darcy. And you, Coleslaw, please relax. Nothing is going to happen to you, absolutely nothing! We're all simply coming to the end of a grand adventure, and I'm eager to know how you found us out."

"Blanche—" muttered Dan Alexander.

She waved a hand airily. "I must *know*, Dan! *We* must know, for later. We know that you sneaked into my house, Darcy, as I said. We know that little Coleslaw followed Dan one night, and saw him bring in a tank." She suddenly lashed out, "It wasn't very clever of you, Mr. Alexander, to hide that tank in the sand! If you hadn't done that, perhaps the children would never have noticed—"

"Your fault, Blanche!" he gave Mrs. Guizot a terrible look. "I told you it should have been a different type of container. Any fool knows that diving isn't done from a surfboard—even children!" He added viciously, "I told you a disguise wasn't necessary, either—*you* insisted. You had to steal that sketch this kid drew. You had to talk to them, and get involved. You're crazy, Blanche!"

He looked away, breathing hard, obviously terribly angry.

Mrs. Guizot tried to smile, not responding to his attack. "What we don't know," she said to Dash in a high voice, "is how or why you suspected that my *friend*, Dan, and Mr. Herrick might be the same man."

"Uh—" Dash quivered, but they were both looking hard at her, and JC gave a little, tight nod, as if saying "Tell them!"

"Uh—it was his elbow," Dash confessed.

"Elbow!" Mrs. Guizot exclaimed.

"And the way he stands and walks," JC finally spoke. He sounded hoarse and frightened.

"Elbow!" Mrs. Guizot repeated, looking at Dan Alexander. He was standing in that familiar posture, with one hand propped far in back. "Oh, I see—of course. Dan, it looks so *pointed!* Oh, my word!" She began to laugh hysterically, while Dan Alexander looked at his own arm. "And we never noticed, oh dear! To think that we'd find such observant children here—and an artist like Darcy-Dash. Oh, my word! The best laid plans of mice and men! All that work! And to be found out by two little children!" She laughed and laughed.

"But we didn't tell anybody—about anything!" JC squeaked, still with that insane grin on his face, swallowing and swallowing.

"That's something we don't know and can't trust," said Dan Alexander in a low voice. "You kids have done too much snooping. "You even snooped around here, didn't you?" he added angrily. "I thought you would, and don't deny it. Nobody else prowls around this house."

Dash gulped and caught JC's eyes. So the fallen tank *had* been a trap!

Dan Alexander walked to the painting on the counter and slammed down his fist beside it, looking at Mrs. Guizot. "And you even had to leave *this* for them to find! You're a fool, Blanche!"

"But," Mrs. Guizot laughed unsteadily, "it's part of

the joy of discovery! I told you, Dan, I wanted Darcy to *see*—"

"And I won't tell anybody about it!" cried Dash quickly, sliding to the end of the couch, nearer JC in the chair. She rose, babbling, "*We* won't tell anybody! I mean, it's perfectly natural, isn't it? *Family* paintings—well, it's not exactly like stealing, is it?"

"I'm so glad you understand that, Darcy-Dash," Mrs. Guizot smiled. "I knew you would."

Casually, as if it didn't mean a thing, Dash moved behind JC's chair. "We just had—uh, *fun*, trying to figure out what you were doing. It was just—a game! There was nothing else to do, and of course we wouldn't dream of mentioning it." She tried, surreptitiously, to reach down for JC's bound arms.

"And it's all over now," she hurried on, "and you know everything about us—so I guess it's time to go home—"

Desperately she tried to untie JC. Mrs. Guizot didn't make a move to stop her, she just watched, almost sympathetically. And, as if he had all the time in the world, Dan Alexander walked behind the counter and then out with another length of clothes line.

Watching him come toward her, Dash felt paralyzed again. Everything was in slow motion! Before she could even flail out, or resist, he flipped her on the floor with one swift motion, turned her over, and tied her arms—and feet. His grip was like iron, and the tight cord hurt.

"Gently—gently," she heard Mrs. Guizot's voice as she lay, face down, on the floor.

And then JC's voice as he screamed, and yelled, and

then was silent. Nobody could have heard him outside through the fog. It muffled everything.

Dan Alexander picked Dash up and shoved her back on the couch. JC was still in the chair, but with the handkerchief stuffed in his mouth, and a piece of tape across it.

"Don't you dare!" Dash screamed, and, fog or no fog, started yelling herself.

"Please don't cry out, Darcy," begged Mrs. Guizot. "Dan—perhaps you don't need—"

But he quickly ripped another piece of tape from the roll he held in his hand, and slapped it across her mouth. The only sound she could make was a muffled groan.

"Lousy kids!" he muttered, glaring at Mrs. Guizot.

"Oh dear, I suppose this is partly my fault," she apologized to Dash. "But neither of you are to worry for a moment. This is only temporary while we make our—what do they call it in films?—our 'getaway'!" She patted Dash on her shoulder. "You see, my dear, my father's paintings are quite valuable now, and this *is* a major art theft. We're now—criminals—on the run.

"Did I mention," she added, twinkling, "that my husband actually had to learn cat-burgling to recover the paintings for me? That puts him in a rather awkward position, doesn't it?"

"Blanche!" Dan Alexander warned her threateningly.

"You've upset all our plans!" Mrs. Guizot went on happily to Dash and JC. "But I can't say I'm too sorry. I admire you both for being so clever! We were all in disguise, weren't we?"

Dash tried to tell Mrs. Guizot something with her

eyes. She couldn't speak, not even mumble, only sort of hum behind the tape. It was a horrible feeling! And their own house was so near! This couldn't be happening! She wanted to tell Mrs. Guizot that they couldn't do this—not leave JC and her all tied up like this.

"It won't be long," said Mrs. Guizot, as if she understood. "Tomorrow afternoon at the very latest! By that time we'll be faraway, and I promise to put in a call here to the island. I'll make sure somebody finds you. And I'm terribly sorry, Darcy—Coleslaw—that this is necessary. But it is, you see."

"You'll not make any calls, Blanche," said Dan Alexander softly. Cutting more lengths of cord from the line, he was fixing JC to the chair, and then tied Dash firmly to the couch. "We're not going anywhere."

"Of course we are!" Mrs. Guizot rose to her feet. "We must! That was the plan."

"*Your* plan," he smiled at her in the most terrible way.

Dash shivered all over watching him. Once JC had said, "Suppose he's a really evil person? Suppose he has a gun?" She caught JC's eyes and saw he was thinking the same thing. He was terrified.

Mrs. Guizot herself looked frightened as he quickly advanced upon her. "*I'm* not a fool, Blanche," he whispered with narrowed eyes. "You've paid me handsomely and I intend to use the money as *I* wish. I'm not leaving—not to Mexico or South America—or anywhere. And neither are you."

His voice was like silk as he looked at Dash and JC. "*They* are."

"Not the children!" Mrs. Guizot went white beneath her green, peaked hood. She stood stiffly, not looking at all "crazy" anymore. "Not the children! You can't touch them, Dan! I won't have it!"

JC's eyes bulged, and Dash was thinking the same thing. His dream! Dan Alexander surfing out, and dumping, drowning him in the ocean! And the surfboard was on the deck, and in this fog. . . .

"You won't have it?" he smiled. "You're crazy enough, Blanche, to trust kids not to say anything?"

"Dan!" Mrs. Guizot took a step forward.

"There's absolutely nothing you can do about it, Blanche," his mouth twisted in a smile again.

. . . And then the room exploded!

Feet pounded up the inside stairs. A figure plunged in, paused, looked at Dash and JC tied up and gagged, at Dan Alexander and Mrs. Guizot—and then flew across the room, grabbing for his shoulders.

CANDY! Like a flying Valkyrie, an avenging angel! She grabbed him from behind—he staggered and turned. WHOP! She socked him in the jaw. He recovered, swung at her—she ducked. And came up with a sneakered foot—ZAP! Right under his chin. He crashed to the floor, rose on an elbow, then to his feet, crouched, and came at her. Candy backed, zig-zagging, teasing him on. He swung at her. POW! She got him with a sideways kick again, and he stumbled backward.

Dash didn't believe what she saw! Candy, in action, was like an animated Super-Girl! Bat-Woman! Goddess from Space!

He lurched at her again. BAM! SPLAT! ARRGH!

POW! Candy's arms were like a windmill. Her kicks were too fast to see! BINGO! A punch, a kick, a chop—and he was out, flat on the floor.

Candy stood over him, panting, her flying yellow hair settling on her shoulders.

Dash gurgled under the tape.

Candy ripped it off, untied her, removed JC's gag and untied him. She didn't say a word. She grabbed all the lengths of clothes line, flipped Dan Alexander over with one foot, and tied him up! Then she looked around for a phone.

"Mrs. Guizot!" Dash cried, looking around.

She was gone. The upstairs door was open, and fog swirled into the room. Dash stumbled to the counter. The painting was also gone.

JC hadn't moved from the chair. He was shuddering, making a valiant effort not to cry. But tears rolled down his cheeks as he tried to keep smiling. "Was I braaaaave?" he wailed.

"Terrific!" said Dash, closing the outside door. "But why did you do it?" she shouted at him. "I told you not to sneak in here!"

"It was our last chance," JC sniffled. "And I didn't think it was a real t-t-trap!" He began to bawl in earnest, and Dash sat on the arm of the chair, hugging him.

Candy had found the phone. "Police?" she said briskly.

JC swallowed a sob, and he and Dash stared at their sister in wonder.

"How'd you *know*?" Dash asked Candy two hours later.

They were all at the beach, sitting just below the dunes. Candy had run home to tell Audrey they all wanted to sit "in the fog" for a while. It was as heavy as it had been all day, but the wind was slowly dying. They'd decided not to tell their mother anything tonight. Daddy would be arriving tomorrow, and they could tell them both together. Why have Audrey worry all night long? The police would have yet more questions, and even they had promised to wait for a day.

It was cool outside, and damp, but the sand was warm over Dash's toes. She sat with her arm around JC. On his other side, Candy had her arm around him, too. He'd been in a state of near-shock, but was gradually recovering.

JC had sneaked in and gone upstairs, just like Dash, and had also discovered the tank and painting. But he'd been grabbed quickly by Dan Alexander who held him outside, on the top deck, until Dash ventured in. Mrs. Guizot had insisted upon replacing the painting for Dash to find.

"Why did he allow her to do that?" she wondered aloud. "He seemed so angry about it."

"He didn't care by then," JC quavered. "I think h-h-he was going to bump her off, too."

JC's experience had been worse than Dash's, because he hadn't really known what was going on. Mrs. Guizot hadn't explained anything to him; she'd waited for Dash. So Dash had to tell JC, and Candy, and the police, the whole story.

Before the police took Dan Alexander off in their jeep down the beach, he had "squealed," too, hoping to place all the blame on Mrs. Guizot. She hadn't succeeded in making her "getaway" with the painting. She'd been picked up, an hour ago, while trying to hire a private water-taxi to cross the bay.

Now they knew everything—almost. Except how Candy had managed to arrive in the nick of time! How Candy had ever learned her incredible combination of Karate, Kung-Fu, Judo, and plain old boxing!

"How did you *know*?" Dash repeated. "I mean, how did you know where we were?"

"Oh, you don't want to hear that," said Candy.

"Yes, we do!" said Dash and JC together. "Tell us."

"Well, I knew you were gone, in the fog, and I figured something creepy was up."

"But how'd you know *where* to look for us?" they asked.

Candy sighed in the fog. "That's what you really don't want to know."

"Yes, we do!"

"You're not going to like this," said Candy. "I knew where you were, because you're such lousy detectives."

They were both completely still. And then asked, "*Why*?"

"All you've done for the past few weeks is whisper and slink around and look guilty."

"Were we that obvious?" Dash couldn't believe it.

"Worse!" said Candy. "You were awful. You even had to wrap your leg in those dumb bandages."

"You knew why I put 'em on?" cried Dash.

"It wasn't very hard to figure out," said Candy. "Especially after I found your cartoons with dates and the whole story—"

"You found it! How'd you find it?" Dash and JC yelled together.

"Well, if people have been acting crazy and suspicious, wouldn't you snoop around a little?"

"Sure! That's what we did," said JC. "I mean, with Gizzard and that guy."

"So did I," proclaimed Candy. "It was fun! But, wow, if I had something to hide like those cartoons—I sure wouldn't hide them in such an obvious place."

"JC's mattress—*obvious*?" asked Dash.

"Terribly obvious," sighed Candy. "The very first place I snooped."

"So that's how you knew about the round house!" JC gulped.

"Naturally," said Candy. "I've been looking at those drawings almost every day. So what did I find on the last page tonight? The round house with an open door—and an empty tank inside. Elementary, my dear Watson, elementary!" Candy sounded very pleased with herself.

"Wow!" said JC.

"And to think," said Dash, thinking of the painting inside the tank, "that Mrs. Guizot had to do all that, just to get her own father's work. I wonder what they'll do to her."

"Not too much, probably," said Candy. "They'll take that into consideration, and her age, too."

"I wonder what *he* would have done to us," JC shuddered, "if you hadn't come along."

"I don't know," said Candy. "And you know something? I don't want to know! I was *scared*!"

"You, too?" JC asked happily.

"But where'd you learn all that stuff!" cried Dash. "I've never seen anything like it."

"I have no idea," said Candy in a amazed tone herself. "I didn't even know I knew it."

They all remembered the police arriving, seeing Dan Alexander trussed up on the floor, and then gazing at Candy in awe. They'd looked at her powerful shoulders, strong arms, athletic legs, and breathed, "Whew!"

"I just don't know," Candy repeated in the dark. "It was all—just *there*, when I needed it."

JC started to sob a bit again. "Th—thanks for rescuing us, Candy—"

"Aw!" she blurted, "don't thank me! Don't! It's embarrassing. And really, I should thank *you*."

"What for?" asked Dash.

"For showing me what I'm going to do—and be," said Candy. "From now on, I think you two should stick to art and acting, and leave the detecting to me."

"You're going to be a detective?" cried JC.

"Why not?" Candy laughed. "You two are lousy at it, but I'm pretty good! I'll work my way up slowly, first becoming a policeperson."

"WOW! BLAM! SPLAT! POWIE!" sighed Dash. "You'll be terrific, Candy."

It was getting very cold in the sand and it was time to go home.

20

LATER, EVERYTHING appeared in the newspapers. French papers, New York papers, local Long Island papers, and of course in the Fire Island News.

Candy became a heroine. She walked about in a glow of self-confidence as the summer went on. She rose at dawn to go fishing with Eric. She jogged a mile along the beach everyday. She took sailing lessons, lifeguard lessons, and grew, if possible, even taller and stronger as she prepared for her future career. And she didn't scowl or look sour so much—mostly she smiled.

The papers treated Dash and JC rather dismally, they thought. Instead of being applauded for being so observant and perceptive—which they had really expected—they were regarded as bright, attractive, but foolish kids who hadn't had the sense to *tell anyone!* Dire warnings were given to children, not to attempt anything like this all on their own. And to parents unluckly enough to have such headstrong, willful offspring! It made them feel very small.

"Headstrong—willful?" Dash asked JC. "Are we really?"

"Naw!" he grumbled. "We're terrific! They're just nuts!"

"I told you we should tell someone!" Dash would argue.

"And if we had, something worse might have happened!" JC would argue back, and point out correctly, "And Candy wouldn't have had her great adventure!"

Even Dash's cartoon calendar of events was treated with a slight contempt, as something "a kid would do." After she first read that, when no reporter had even *seen* the calendar, but only heard about it, Dash hid it away again. This time securely locked in a suitcase! She was in agony for a few days, thinking that Mr. Hildenbrand might see all this "news."

Audrey was horrified to learn what the children had done. When their father arrived to be innundated by the story, he was at first shocked, but then, as everyone was out of danger, he began to regard it rather like a play.

Daddy first just sat on the deck, listening, then loafing for the next few days. He grew to look quite like Dash's sketch of the Fire Island Freak; unbuttoned, unshaven, shaggy, dazed and euphoric to leave the cares of the world behind. He just stared at the sea, and then drifted out to the beach, sinking into the sand and sun just like Audrey. In a strange way, they both began to resemble the beach, Dash thought.

He'd brought out bicycles for everyone. Candy rode hers so hard it squeaked with complaints. When Dash's leg was completely healed, she rode with JC to Dunewood, along the broad boardwalks of Saltaire, on to Kismet, and back again.

When they weren't riding they were swimming, or flying kites, or roaming over the beach, or fooling around the bay. They met more children than they'd ever met in one place before. Kids lined up for the movies at the Fire House, fifty or sixty at a time. At their house, the screen door was always banging, they had endless sleep-overs, and nobody even had to ask!

The house was always messy and full of sand, and nobody cared. They wore what they wished and nobody pestered them about being neat or clean. They were always clean anyway, if rather salty, from being in and out of the water. They went to bed when they wished and got up when they wanted to. There were no set times for being here and there, except for dinner, once a day.

Altogether it was the most unregulated, sloppy, casual, glorious summer the children had ever known! Oh, Fire Island—heaven!

Toward the end of the summer Audrey decided upon something new. After a lot of thought, she announced one day, "I am not going to write short pieces or work as an editor this fall. Instead, I'm going to write a best selling book and *buy* a house right here on the beach!"

"What kind of book?" everyone asked.

"The kind that sells best, of course—a mystery," she grinned. "And you know what about!"

Dash and JC looked at each other.

"Great Falcon," she said.

"Great Elephant Brain," he said.

"Great Detective Candace Littlewood!" their mother said, and they blinked at each other miserably.

Candy, it was always Candy now, and people seemed to have forgotten what they'd done. Or, thought Dash, they didn't want to be reminded. "Children!" she'd heard some other parents say, "Getting themselves into such danger!" And they would quickly change the subject.

It was the only bad note of their summer, and even Candy thought it was unfair. Otherwise everything was better than perfect. And in late August, even that changed. The Littlewoods got a stunning surprise.

A letter arrived from the museum in France, offering Dash and JC a *reward* for their part in recovering the paintings! With it was a note from the insurance company, explaining that they and the museum director were working this out together.

"It's about time!" Candy shrieked, as thrilled as Dash and JC! "I thought you were going to be ignored forever!"

Carefully, in not very skillful English, the director wrote that without "les enfants terrible et adroit"—the one French phrase he used—Roger Prudhomme's work might have been lost forever. As they were still so young, he was inquiring of Monsieur and Madame Littlewood whether a sum toward future education would be appropriate? Or, would they prefer to consider an expense-paid trip to France whenever possible?

"A trip! A trip!" yelled Dash and JC, beside themselves with joy.

But later, Dash grew sad, thinking of Mrs. Guizot. They weren't sure where she was now, or what had happened to her. Dan Alexander was in jail, and the round house had been rented to a group of people for the summer. The last they'd heard of Mrs. Guizot, she was supposed to be sent back to France with her husband, as they were both guilty of stealing the paintings.

Her own father's paintings! Was that really so awful, Dash sometimes wondered? She got a knot in her throat when she thought of it. Why hadn't he left her anything? Of course, he hadn't known what a great artist he was; he probably hadn't meant to cut her off, he'd simply given his work to the world.

She hadn't any brothers or sisters, that had come out in the papers—Mrs. Guizot was an only child. Of course, she'd want something of his. But to rob the museum of *all* those works? And she hadn't planned to sell them, just to keep them, to have them surrounding her. If she just wanted to look at them, why couldn't she have stayed in France, and gone to see them as part of the world?

Her husband was a wealthy man, too. They could have tried to trace those friends of her father; tried to buy back some paintings. But they'd made no effort. Maybe her husband had enjoyed the adventure of "burgling." Maybe Mrs. Guizot hadn't wanted the "world" to have her father's work. Maybe, as JC said, she really was a greedy person. Or a hurt person somehow. Dash felt sorry for her.

But she didn't feel sorry for Dan Alexander! He was languishing in jail, and deserved it, Dash thought. A really evil person. Eric had been amazed, as well as everyone else who learned about him. No, his plight didn't bother her in the least. Only Mrs. Guizot did, whenever she thought about art.

Dash would never forget that painting by Roger Prudhomme—never! How had he seen all that, and conveyed it in such an extraordinary way? Not just a landscape, but something more that included the large and small together. . . .

His other paintings had been taken to an apartment in New York City by Dan Alexander in that briefcase, just as she and JC thought, and were now back in the museum. Where she would be able to see them one day, she and JC.

Dash didn't draw anymore, after that awful night! She couldn't really take credit for not drawing; the thought of it, and of her cartoon calendar, made her sick. So did remembering Mrs. Guziot's talk about her work. Dash had to acknowledge the awful fact that although old "Gizzard" hadn't wanted them "bumped off," as JC said, she had still planned to leave them there in the round house, all trussed up, for an entire night and day! That wasn't very nice of her!

She didn't draw one line, and didn't even suffer from not drawing! Mr. Hildebrand would be proud of her. Nothing went on a piece of paper all during July and

August, until, at the very end of the summer, something happened.

It was their last day at Fair Harbor, and it looked like the most beautiful day of all. Dash woke very early, before anyone else was awake. Outside the blue ocean rolled, the white caps sparkled—and Dash almost cried. She couldn't stand the thought of leaving.

She looked around the porch, at the bicycles jammed against a wall, the fishing pole, crab net, flippers, kites, the games and comic books and playing cards, all to be packed today. She wanted to stay here forever!

She walked out on deck to an incredible sight. Hundreds—no, thousands of butterflies were flying and landing everywhere. The deck, the roof, the sky, the dunes, were filled with them! They fluttered from the northeast on gusts of wind, moving erratically down the shoreline. Dash ran to the end of the deck and looked toward the bay. They were on telephone wires, the rooftops of every house, lovely black and orange creatures with wings trembling in the wind. They flew, and landed, and flew again.

Dash ran down the ramp, and then over and down the dune steps to the beach. They were flying over the sand, landing to rest near the waves, before fluttering on again. She'd never seen anything so lovely, so magical—it was like a fairy-tale world, a fantasy!

She lay down flat and very quietly to watch one single butterfly resting on a small hill of sand. Its wings rose, fell, trembled, and fluttered like a pulse. She watched it, hardly breathing, until it rose again and flew away. Another came to take its place, and above her head, the air was filled with movement. She ran back to the house under a canopy of butterflies, and without thinking of anything, pulled out a sketch pad from one of the bags.

Then pencils, magic markers, water colors. She sat at the old table on the porch and sketched, then got a jar of water from the kitchen. She used the water colors, then some magic markers, crayons, a darker pencil—a hodge-podge of different mediums.

Dash didn't even know that JC was standing behind her until he said, "You've never done anything like that before!"

She was so quietly engrossed he didn't even startle her. "I guess I haven't," she blinked, trying to see what she'd really done.

"If that dumb art teacher of yours says anything bad about this, well—lead me to him!" said JC. "On the other hand, you haven't been drawing for two months. Do you really think that has anything to do with it?"

They looked at what she'd done together.

The butterfly seemed alive, resting, breathing on the sand. The strong colors of the magic markers did something to the soft, pale water colors. They shouldn't have worked together—but they did. And the pencil shadings made the butterfly "important" in some way. It seemed very large, although there was an impression of its real size. It was one of the strangest drawings-paintings Dash had ever seen. She liked it! Even if she had done it . . . herself.

"It's really good, isn't it?"

"Fantastic!" said JC. "Hey—I just found out about the butterflies. It's an annual migration of Monarchs.

Just like birds. The fellow in the next house said we're lucky to see it."

· *See—seeing.* Dash stared at her work. She could certainly show this to Hildy! She'd finally "seen" something besides a pointed elbow and a "bushy bear man."

"Ohhh, JC!" she sighed enormously. "What a summer!"

"What a *fall*!" he crowed. "I'm ready!"

She turned in her chair to look at him.

"Don't you think Pierre L'Enfant's a good name for a French Detective?" JC grinned.

He was sure "ready"! JC had decked himself out in his only good-for-going-out tan Bermuda shorts, a pair of his father's knee-high navy-blue socks which rose from old red sneakers, a red and yellow striped T-shirt, and his only good brown corduroy blazer. His father's Irish tweed cap was set smartly, at a cocky angle, atop his straggly hair. In one hand JC held his father's black briefcase, and in the other an enormous magnifying glass!

Dash rolled, then crossed her eyes, and then saluted him. "But who'll I be?" she asked.

"Who else?" JC bowed sweepingly. "Marie Mata Hari Antoinette L'Enfant!"

His gestures were magnificent, his accent was faultless. A perfect Huckleberry Finn turned French Detective on their very last day at Fire Island. It made leaving a whole lot easier.

"Hey, JC—I love you!" Dash grinned back.

"Yeah, I kind of like you, too," said JC.

She couldn't help it. She turned to another page in her book, and, giggling, started to sketch him.

About the Author

Hope Campbell was born in Seattle, Washington and attended private schools in California, Hawaii, and China. Since her early teens she has been an actress, appearing in Los Angeles, New York, and throughout Europe. She has worked for radio and television and even in a three-ring circus!

Though she began writing as a sideline to her acting, she has published over 14 books, including an ALA Best Book for Young Adults, in addition to several short stories. She has two children and currently lives in New York City.